Also by Kelly Oram

Being Jamie Baker
More Than Jamie Baker

Serial Hottie
V is for Virgin
Chameleon

For Mom, my favorite science geek.

Avery

The following journal is a scientific study on the process of overcoming heartbreak and is my official entry for the 2013 Utah State Science Fair.

My theory is that having your heart broken is very similar to experiencing the death of a loved one. Therefore, it stands to reason that by using the commonly accepted seven stages of grief (shock/disbelief, denial, bargaining, guilt, anger, depression, and acceptance/hope), one can overcome the devastating effects of a broken heart.

In this experiment, I will prove my theory by taking you through the seven stages of grief as applied to my own severely-damaged heart. I hypothesize that once I have experienced all seven of these steps, I will have cured my heart of all cracks and tears and will be otherwise ready to fall in love again.

As I, Avery Shaw—average sixteen-year-old junior in Spanish Fork, Utah—am obviously not impartial on this topic and will not always be able to make unbiased observations, I have recruited the help of fellow Spanish Fork High student Grayson Kennedy to be an objective outside observer throughout this study. Unlike me, the eighteen-year-old basketball star and womanizing socialite has absolutely no personal interest in the outcome of this experiment. (He's in it for the extra credit.)

We call this project The Avery Shaw Experiment.

shock and disbelief

Avery

To really grasp the full extent of the shock I experienced when Aiden Kennedy broke my heart, you need to understand the unusual circumstances of our relationship up until that point.

Aiden and I had known each other since birth. Our mothers met in a prenatal yoga class and became instant best friends, bonding over the same due date and a mutual tendency to throw up during class.

Aiden and I were born on the same cold winter day: February 11, 1997. As babies we went to all the same playdates and mommy-and-me groups. When we got a little older, it became the same preschool and then the same elementary school, middle school, and high school. We have all the same friends, participate in all the same extracurricular activities, and have even celebrated every single one of our birthdays together.

I'd been desperately in love with Aiden for years, but despite my secret undying devotion, we'd never been anything but the very best of friends. Knowing boys are slower to develop in the romance department, I waited patiently for Aiden to catch up to my feelings. I never had any doubt that he would one day see me for the girl I am and give me my first kiss. Then we would go to prom together and eventually end up as Mr. and Mrs. Aiden and Avery Kennedy. Even our names fit perfectly together.

Aiden dropped the bomb that changed my life this past New Year's Eve. My mom and I had gone—as we did every year—with the Kennedy family up to their insanely nice condo in Park City for winter break. It was nearing dinnertime, and Aiden and I were watching this fascinating documentary about the effects of steroid use on the human body.

"Where in the world is your brother?" Aiden's mom, Cheryl, stood in the kitchen, frowning at the pile of dishes in the sink.

Grayson Kennedy is not my brother, technically, but I didn't think twice before answering his mom's question. "He went downstairs to the gym about an hour ago."

"Shirtless," Aiden added with a snort. "I guess the new tenants down in 7B have a good-looking daughter. What was the term he used?"

"Whooty." I laughed.

"Whooty?" Cheryl echoed.

"It was a new one for us too. We had to look it up."

Aiden happily recited the definition we'd read on Urbandictionary.com. "'A white girl who has a pretty face, a nice slim waist, and a voluptuously large, bountiful, beautiful booty'."

Cheryl let out a long, exasperated sigh, yet there was a hint of amusement in her voice when she said, "Where does he come up with that stuff?"

As if he'd felt his ears burning, Grayson burst through the front door and answered his mom's question. "Some people just have a gift." He trounced into the kitchen—still shirtless and now drenched in sweat—scooped his mom up into a big hug, and plastered a sloppy kiss on her cheek. "Love you, Mom! What's for dinner? I'm starving."

"Gross!" Cheryl shrieked and slapped him away. "That is disgusting, Grayson! I know I've taught you better manners than that!"

Grayson frowned. "Since when is hugging your mom and telling her you love her bad manners?"

Cheryl sighed again but cracked a smile. She shoved a chocolate-chip cookie into her oldest son's mouth after seeing the pout on his face.

Some people have gifts all right. Grayson Kennedy could charm the pants off of any girl he met, and frequently did if the rumors around school were to be believed. Which they were.

"I love you too, honey," Cheryl said, "but you stink. Go shower, please, and then get in here and do these dishes."

"The dishes?" Grayson whined, heading for the fridge.

Thankfully Cheryl intercepted the milk and handed Grayson a glass before he could slobber all over the carton. "Yes. The dishes. It was your turn to do them after lunch. If they're not done before dinner, then you will be in charge of all the dinner dishes as well, and Avery will be off the hook tonight."

"Sweet," I called over my shoulder from the living room. "By all means, Grayson, put it off a little longer."

Grayson finally noticed Aiden and I on the couch. "What are you two dorks doing?"

"Learning about steroids," I said cheerfully. "You should probably know that using them can cause acne, testicular atrophy, decreased sperm count, prostate enlargement, and gynecomastia."

Grayson looked rightfully appalled. "Gyneco-what-ia?"

"Enlarged breasts in men," Aiden translated. "So you should lay off the juice before you have to start borrowing Avery's bras."

I gasped at the mention of my underwear and whacked Aiden's shoulder hard.

Behind me, Grayson laughed. I knew he was about to deliver a comeback, but I refused to look at him. Seconds later his breath was warm on my neck. He whispered just low enough that his mother couldn't hear what he said. "I like my bras colorful and lacy, Aves. Not sure your collection would do it for me."

Total mortification. Grayson may be as close as family to me, but he was still one of the hottest, most popular guys in our whole school. He, discussing my bras in that low, sexy voice that could stop a girl's heart on the spot, made my lungs constrict. Plus, he was right of course. My bras were all of the plain white cotton variety.

"Mom! Grayson's picking on Avery again!"

Aiden's shout startled me back from my panic attack. Grayson was still watching me, a wicked smile playing on his lips, so I did the only thing I could think to do. I sniffed once and then pretended to gag. "Ugh. Your mom's right. You really reek. Please go sweat all over someone else."

Grayson laughed his way back into the kitchen in search of more cookies.

"What is it that makes your brother a walking hormone?" I asked Aiden. "Is it all the physical activity, you think? I mean with the working out, the snowboarding, and the basketball, he's got to be on an endorphin high like, what, eighty-five percent of the time? Do you think there's a correlation between the two? Like the more active the athlete, the bigger the sex-craved maniac?"

Aiden shrugged. "Probably. Think about the reputations of professional athletes."

"Ha! Maybe that should be the topic of our experiment for science club this year."

Aiden gave me a weird look. "How, exactly, would you go about testing that theory?"

I thought about the practical application that would be required for an experiment like that and promptly blushed again.

"Fine," I relented, though the thought of Aiden and me working up a sweat together only to then go work up another one with a hot make-out session was highly appealing. "But we need to come up with something soon. The fair is in March this year. It doesn't give us a lot of time."

Aiden's entire body suddenly went stiff. I glanced at him just in time to watch his face turn a little green.

"What's the matter with you?" I wanted to make a joke about him being strung out due to steroids or something, but he looked too freaked to tease. Something was really wrong with him, so I paused the TV, sat up straight and gave him my full attention.

"Are you okay?"

"Yeah." Aiden gulped. "It's just…I've been meaning to talk to you about that."

"About what?"

He took a big breath and then let it out. "I'm not going to do the science fair this year."

It took a minute for this news to sink in. We'd been partners at the Utah State Science Fair every year since sixth grade.

"What?"

"Um…well…Miles Fuller moved over break, so the debate team needs one more person or they won't be able to compete anymore. Mindy Perez and I had public speaking together last semester. She asked me to fill Miles's spot. She said I have charisma and a natural talent for persuasion."

I couldn't talk for a full sixty seconds. He was speaking

English, but I still couldn't make sense of his words. "You joined the debate team?"

He nodded.

"But they meet at the same time as science club."

"I know." Aiden's gaze dropped to his lap as if he could no longer stand to look at me. "I quit science club. I already emailed Mr. Walden about it."

"You *quit?*" My voice jumped so many octaves that it broke halfway through the word quit. It had the unpleasant effect of making me sound like a mouse. "But you're my co-president!"

"You're better with all the science stuff than me anyway."

"Yeah, but I'm not like, a leader. That's why the gang voted us both. Together. I *need* you."

Aiden winced and then forcefully shook his head. "You don't."

"Fine," I said, even though it felt very, very *not* fine. "But even if you quit, you could still do the science fair with me. Everyone's already partnered up. I'll have to do it alone."

Aiden finally met my eyes. He looked even guiltier now. "I won't have time. Mindy said debate gets pretty intense. Plus with all the honors courses we have this semester? The science fair is a lot of work."

"I know! And we've already waited until January to get started. I won't be able to do it by myself. I'll have to drop out."

"No, you won't," Aiden insisted. "You're amazing, Avery. You'll find a way. You always do. And hey, without me bringing you down, you'll probably win first place for once."

"Shut up! I will not! I will fall apart without you!"

Aiden sighed and took my hand in his. "Aves," he said slowly. "That's also sort of why I said yes to Mindy. I think I need a little space for a while."

For just a brief moment, time stopped...like a heart that skipped a beat. When it started back up, my life had been forever altered.

"Space? What do you mean?" I knew what he meant. I was just praying I was wrong because, otherwise, he'd just ripped my heart in two and I couldn't deal. "Are you saying you don't want to be my friend anymore?"

Aiden quickly shook his head. "Of course not. We'll always be friends. You know we will. But, Aves, we spend more time together than conjoined twins. I think it would be good for us both to maybe start hanging out with other people sometimes, you know? Like, separately. And..." Another shrug, and painful swallow. "I don't want to celebrate our birthdays together this year. I kind of want to do my own thing."

At that last request there was a gasp and the sound of shattering glass in the kitchen. I was grateful for the distraction until I realized that Cheryl was standing there practically comatose staring at us with a hand over her mouth and tears in her eyes. The gasp had been hers, and the glass of water she'd been holding was now on the ground around her bare feet in as many tiny pieces as my heart was.

"Mom!" Aiden jumped up and started picking up the larger pieces of glass.

I went to get a dish towel and the broom, but my movements were robotic. My body was on autopilot because my brain was pretty much dead from shock.

I simply couldn't understand how this had happened. Was the earth suddenly tilted off its axis? Were the boundaries of space and time blurring, causing reality to splinter off into alternate universes? Was Park City, Utah, secretly the Devil's Gate and I'd fallen into hell without knowing it?

I handed Aiden the towel and then swept up the remaining glass, but when I went to dump the dustpan, I accidentally ran into a wall of solid, sweaty muscles. "Sorry," I muttered to Grayson.

He was standing there shifting his eyes between his brother and me, with unswallowed chocolate-chip cookie bits threatening to fall out of his gaping mouth.

"Can you get out of the way? You're blocking the trash can."

This made him jump into action. "Oh, right. Sorry." He stepped aside and fled the kitchen muttering something about needing to take a shower.

I watched him go because it was easier than facing his brother.

From behind me, Aiden's fingers gently grabbed onto mine. "Aves."

His soft voice made my eyes burn. He tugged lightly on my hand, but I couldn't turn around yet. I was about to cry, and there was no way I was going to let him see that.

"Avery."

After a nice deep breath, the burning sensation

subsided. I was able to face him and force a smile, but I think my injured pride was the only thing that kept the tears at bay.

"You okay?" Aiden asked.

The answer was a definite no, but I nodded anyway. "Of course. Yeah, sure, I'm fine. Why wouldn't I be? It's just a science project. Like you said, I'll manage. As for the other stuff, I get it, and that's cool. If that's what you want. I suppose it could be fun to change things up a bit."

Lie! Complete and utter lie!

The lie was so big it hurt me all the way to my soul, but what hurt even worse was that Aiden believed it. He let out a breath and then threw his arms around me. His whole body sagged with relief. "I am so glad you understand. I was so scared that you were going to hate me for this and never speak to me again."

"I could never to that," I muttered.

His grip tightened gratefully, but he may as well have been reaching inside my chest and squeezing the last of the life out of my heart instead of hugging me.

I pinched my eyes shut. I was going to lose it. The tears weren't going to stay back forever. I had minutes, maybe seconds, left before I fell apart.

"It's fine," I insisted again as I pulled out of Aiden's embrace. "You know I could never hate you."

Aiden sent me a megawatt smile. "Thanks, Aves." He kissed my cheek and whispered, "You're the best."

I couldn't speak now without giving myself away, so I just nodded.

Cheryl must have recognized the truth of my emotional state, because she cleared her throat and asked Aiden if he wouldn't mind taking the garbage bag with all the broken glass out to the dumpster.

Cheryl threw her arms around me the second he was gone. "Avery, I am so sorry! So, so sorry! I don't understand…" She let her voice trail off. She was every bit as bewildered as I was.

"It's okay, Cheryl. It's fine. Really." I pushed away from her and practically ran out of the room. I only made it to the upstairs hallway before I collapsed to the floor and cried.

A few minutes later the door downstairs slammed. I sucked in a deep breath, knowing I needed to at least make it to my room before Aiden rounded the corner and saw me, but it was my mother's voice I heard, not Aiden's.

Her jovial "Grayson! Avery! Go help Aiden bring up the groceries!" was not repeated like it normally would have been when neither of us responded. Instead, I could hear a few hushed whispers and then one very loud, startled gasp. Cheryl had just spilled the beans to my mother, and they were no doubt discussing how destroyed I was.

I scrambled to my feet when I heard my mom say "I'll go talk to her. Maybe I'll take her out just the two of us for New Year's Eve tonight."

No way did I want to do that. I loved my mom and all, but I wasn't ready to face the truth yet. I was in way too much shock. Stage one of the grieving process? Currently underway.

I also didn't need a special pity party tonight while the

Kennedy family pretended like they didn't know why mom and I ditched them.

In a panic I burst through the first door I could find and backed up against it. I'd been known to have an anxiety attack or two in my time, but I'd never experienced one quite as bad as this. My head was swimming, every part of my body hurt, I couldn't breathe, and I couldn't think straight.

I was so out of it that I'd slipped into the bathroom while Grayson was in the shower, and I didn't even notice until he poked his head out from behind the curtain with a surprised look on his face. "Aves, babe, I'm a little busy here." He cocked an eyebrow and gave me a crooked smile. "Unless you're planning to join me…?"

Just then there was a loud knock on the door, and my mother's worried voice called out to me. I looked up at Grayson and in a moment of sheer panic didn't think twice before jumping behind the curtain with him.

"Whoa! Avery! I was only teasing!"

I could hear Grayson, but I couldn't really respond. I leaned my back against the cold tile wall and closed my eyes, letting the hot water rain down on me.

There was another knock, louder this time, and then the door opened. "Avery? That you in here, sweetie?"

I frantically shook my head, praying that Grayson would do the right thing.

"Sorry, Kaitlin. It's just me."

"Oh. Sorry, Grayson. I thought maybe you were Avery."

"Yeah, I get that a lot," he teased.

My mom laughed and then sighed heavily. "If you see her after you're done, tell her I'm looking for her."

"Will do."

The door clicked shut and things got quiet. I stood there for so long that my head started to hurt and I got really dizzy. My knees buckled.

Grayson quickly caught me under the arms. "Avery, breathe," he commanded.

I took a breath. As oxygen flooded my lungs, I realized it was probably the first breath I'd taken in minutes. Literally.

"Aves," a low steady voice said. I felt hands on either side of my face.

I opened my eyes, and Grayson's beautiful piercing blue ones were staring down at me from just inches away, taking up my entire field of vision. "You good now?" he asked.

I may have been breathing, but I would never be "good" again. I flung my arms around him and began to release gut-wrenching sobs into his chest.

I have no idea how long I stayed like that, holding onto Grayson for dear life while I shattered from the inside out. However long it was, Grayson never tried to stop me. He held me close and rocked me beneath the spray of the hot water, all the while whispering encouraging sentiments to me and stroking my hair.

Eventually the anxiety attack faded, and I regained control of myself. Of course, that's when I realized I was standing in the shower clinging to a very naked Grayson Kennedy and that certain parts of him were not objecting to the situation.

I gasped and tried to wrench myself away from him, but he held me tight and chuckled. "It is what it is, Aves. I'm a warm-blooded guy standing naked in a shower, holding a girl whose t-shirt is drenched and clinging rather poetically to her surprisingly impressive figure."

This time when I gasped, Grayson let me go. He was still laughing long after I scrambled out of the tub. I didn't feel bad when I stole his towel and left him to fend for himself when he was ready to get out.

(Yeah, you read that right. If Avery gets one of these nifty prologue thingies to explain herself, then so do I. She's not the only one with a story to tell here!)

Grayson

First of all, let the record show that journals are completely lame. I'll probably get gyneco-whatever-it-was just for owning the stupid thing.

Secondly—and this is the more important point I need to make in my one-of-a-kind-totally-brilliant extra prologue—Avery's experiment is a load of crap.

Avery Shaw is not really suffering from an actual broken heart. Oh, she's hurt for true. No doubt my idiot little brother messed her up good, for which he will receive a proper beating someday, I promise you that. But Avery was not really in love with Aiden and, therefore, is not suffering from a true broken heart.

What Avery is really suffering from is a heaping load of rejection and a detrimental dose of codependence.

Avery and Aiden are a truly whacked-out case. Our moms screwed them both out of any chance at normalcy long before they were ever born. Of course Avery loves Aiden, but she has no freaking clue what it means to be *in* love with someone. She only thinks she does. Her perspective is unbelievably skewed in the direction of Crazytown.

To Avery, Aiden is familiar and safe. She translates those feelings of security into being in love with him because it's easier than seeing them for what they really are—a crutch she uses to cope with her shyness and social anxiety issues.

So, you see, her theory that she is going to magically cure herself by experiencing the seven stages of grief is total bull. Luckily, she has a partner on this project that is not as dumb as everyone thinks he is. I am going to fix her with an experiment of my own.

While Avery is going through her deluded journey of getting over my brother—which, again, I am fully supportive of and will do whatever work she needs me to—I will be doing all the *real* work behind the Avery Shaw Experiment.

When I'm through with her, Avery Shaw will be a fully-functional, beautiful, self-confident, emotionally-stable young woman who is ready to experience actual real love, with or without her precious seven stages of grief.

Also, my baby brother will forever regret the day he made the stupidest mistake of his life.

an experiment is born

Grayson

Where does one even begin when talking about Avery Shaw? I've known her, her whole life, and yet I've never really gotten to know her.

She and her mom have been unofficial members of my family since our moms threw up on each other in a prenatal yoga class when I was fourteen months old. They only got closer after Avery's dad skipped town when Avery was four. My family sort of adopted them, and my father took his place as the only male role model in Avery's life.

I always looked at her as sort of a pesky little sister, but that all changed the day my brother dumped her. Why, you ask? Let me put it this way: When a girl lets you be the one to hold her as her entire world falls apart, even though you're *ass naked*, it changes the way you see her.

The soaking-wet, see-through t-shirt didn't hurt, either.

It took me a while to get out of the shower after Avery finally left. I had to let the water run cold first because, well, because I had to. Plus, I needed some time to process. Avery Shaw had suddenly barged into so much more than just my shower. She'd also crashed into my head in a way I never thought possible and maybe even wormed her way into my heart a little bit. I had no freaking clue how to handle that, much less what to do about it. But I had to do *something*. Avery was destroyed and completely incapable of fixing herself.

That was the moment the Avery Shaw Experiment started for me. It wasn't defined yet, and I had no idea I'd be earning extra credit for it—that was an added bonus—but that was the first time I realized Avery Shaw had the potential to be so much more than what she was. All she needed was a little help from someone normal and cool who could introduce her to life the way it's supposed to be lived.

I decided, as I cooled off in the shower that day, that I was going to fix Avery Shaw. I was going to help her get over her dependency on my brother and turn her into a normal, socially-competent person by showing her how the world really worked.

I was going to start by making her celebrate New Year's Eve the right way—at a real party, on a real date, with a real kiss at midnight. I was excited about it too. No joke, when

I got dressed that night, I looked in the mirror and was like, "Watch out, Avery Shaw. Grayson Kennedy is about to change your life."

Well somebody had to.

No surprise, I found her in bed buried deep beneath the covers. I sat down near the head-shaped end of the lump under the quilt, and her croaky all-cried-out voice said, "Please, just go away, Mom. I don't want to talk about it right now."

I don't know why, but that made me smile. "Good, because listening really isn't one of my strong points."

I could practically feel the horror radiating out of her when she realized it was me. "Go away, Grayson!" she shrieked. "Haven't I already seen enough of you for one night?"

I've always teased her about the boy/girl stuff because it's too easy to make Little Miss Prude blush. But had the girl always been so hilariously cute?

"You had your eyes closed the entire time," I teased. "You didn't see anything interesting."

"Well, I definitely *felt* it!"

I laughed again. I knew I should probably drop it, but I couldn't help myself. "I'm well aware of what you felt, Aves. I was feeling plenty right then too. Obviously. So, was it as good for you as it was for me?"

"Ugh! You really are made of hormones! Just go away and let me die!"

I backed off before she had a stroke. "No can do, girlie. There's a wild New Year's Eve party over at the resort with our names on it."

I knew she wouldn't say anything, but I paused and gave her the chance anyway before I said, "Unless you'd rather spend the evening with the 'rents and my idiot little brother, drowning in awkward silences and avoiding all eye contact, because you know there is no way our moms will let you hide out in this room all night. I heard them discussing removal strategies not two minutes ago."

I actually hadn't, but I was sure that's what they were doing.

Avery knew it was true too, because she threw the covers off her face and glared at me.

"Come on, Aves. Let's go before they make us do the dishes."

Slowly her glare faded into a wary look. "I don't really have anything to wear to a party."

I'd seen Avery in everything from jeans to pajamas to dresses to swimsuits, but as I let my eyes slide over her then, it was as if I was seeing her for the first time.

Avery's never going to win the award for hottest girl in school, but she's definitely cute. She seems tiny compared to my hulking six-foot-four, hundred-and-eighty-five-pound self, but I think standing next to each other, we have the same effect that a big old golden retriever and a kitten would. Somehow it just works.

She has decent hair—light brown and straight. It goes nicely with her pale skin and light smattering of freckles. She also has a cute little button nose, but her most attractive feature, aside from the amazing rack I'd just discovered, was definitely her big, expressive eyes. They were a vibrant blue very similar to my own, but she never guarded them. You could always see right into her soul. That was the one thing I had always noticed about her before. She was always so honest. All you had to do was look closely and her eyes would tell you everything you wanted to know. That's a rare thing in girls. At least it is in all the ones I've ever dated.

"Just put on whatever you have that's warm," I said.

I started to leave the room, but she stopped me at the door. "Grayson?" Her tone tugged at something inside me. "You really want to take me with you tonight?"

She sounded so small and unsure of herself. It was how she always sounded at school and around strangers but never when she was at home with us. I think my brother had really broken her. I was seriously going to have to beat him sometime.

"You don't have to if you don't want to. I know I really freaked out on you earlier, but I promise I'll be fine. Aiden's right." She swallowed back a lump in her throat. "I'll manage without him somehow."

"Aiden's a tool. You can learn how to manage tomorrow. Tonight's New Year's Eve, and for once in your life, you're going to spend it without Aiden or *The Discovery Channel*."

I knew I was making progress when she cracked a smile and asked, "What about Whootylicious in 7B?"

I thought of the luscious booty I'd originally planned on seeing tonight and sighed. "That *will* be an unfortunate loss, but, like you, I will just have to deal."

I winked and then decided I'd give her ten minutes

before I came back and physically dragged her out of bed.

She didn't make me wait that long. She emerged after only five minutes dressed in a pretty dark-blue sweater dress, skinny jeans, and knee-high black boots. The belt she wore over the sweater showed off her tiny waist and called just the right amount of attention to that glorious chest of hers. Seriously, how had I never noticed that before?

"You look really nice," I blurted, unable to hide my surprise.

The compliment startled her. She blushed and looked at her feet as she mumbled, "I need to blow my hair dry."

I grinned. "Don't want to have to explain to anyone how it got wet, eh?"

She turned even brighter red but then glared at me. "I just don't want my hair to freeze."

I laughed as I threw my hands up in surrender and then laughed even harder when she stalked past me into the bathroom.

I leaned against the door and watched, curiously, as she dried her hair. There was something oddly fascinating about watching Little Avery Shaw primp. She'd never seemed like such a real girl to me before. She wasn't so little anymore, either.

She caught me staring at her in the mirror, so I quickly said, "I thought dorks were supposed to have bad hair and horrible, frumpy fashion senses."

"Just because I enjoy learning doesn't mean I'm a dork," she said, insulted.

"Two words for you Aves: science club."

Avery sucked in a breath, and I realized that the science club might not be the best topic of discussion tonight.

"Words that are no longer allowed to be repeated for the rest of the night," I said quickly. I prayed she wouldn't start crying again.

Avery slowly let the air out of her lungs and then put down the hair dryer. As she brushed her hair into place, I had a strong urge to touch it. Then she coated her lips with a light layer of shiny pink gloss that smelled delicious, and I was the one sucking in a breath. My mouth had suddenly gone dry.

"Okay, I'm ready."

She turned and looked up at me as if wondering what my problem was. Hell if I knew. We shared one small moment of intimacy, and suddenly the girl had my insides turning to mush. She had no idea how close I was to kissing her right then.

"Uh, Grayson?"

"Hmm?"

I pulled my head out of my butt just in time to watch Avery's cheeks get all pink again. Man she was cute like that. "Right. Sorry. Okay. So prepare yourself. Everyone's downstairs, and it's going to be awkward as hell until we can get out the door. Think you can make it?"

She hesitated but then nodded. The action was quick and jerky like a little bit of the panic she felt earlier was creeping back in.

I forced her to keep her eyes focused on me. "Hey. I'm right here. If you need to, just keep your head down and let me do all the talking."

I took her hand when it became apparent that her feet wouldn't start walking on their own. Her fingers automatically curled around mine. She was starting to tremble, so I hurried her downstairs before she had any more time to work herself into another panic attack. I dragged her straight over to the front door, grabbed her coat off the hook, and held it out for her to slip her arms into.

"Where are you guys off to?" my dad asked, being the first one to notice us.

Heads turned our direction and the air in the room turned thick and heavy. I felt the stares every bit as much as Avery did, but I didn't pause in my efforts to bundle her up. I zipped her coat, then reached for her hat and scarf.

"We're just going to go walk around town for a bit, grab some hot cocoa, and maybe head over to the resort in time to catch the fireworks."

Scarf now securely in place, I plopped Avery's hat on her head. Our eyes met and I whispered, "We're almost free. You're doing great." I was shocked when I received a small smile from her.

Avery put on her gloves, while I grabbed my own coat. As I quickly shoved my hat on my head, Aiden finally opened his big, stupid mouth. "You're taking out *Avery?*"

My jaw clenched. I knew it was too much to hope to just get out of there without anyone saying anything. The fact that it was Aiden bringing it up, along with the incredulity in his voice that made it sound as if Avery wasn't good enough to be my date for the evening, pissed me off way more than I'd expected it would.

I felt insanely protective of Avery all a sudden. Instead of just walking out the door like I probably should have, I turned around and gave my brother a defiant look. "Is that a problem?"

Aiden's eyes narrowed on me. "It's just out of character. He flicked his gaze to Avery. "For both of you."

As if he could talk about acting out of character. My hands clenched into fists, matching the tension in my jaw. "You're the one who told her she needed to start hanging out with other people, and since when is it out of character for me to want to spend the evening with a beautiful girl?"

Aiden's face flashed with pure rage, but I stared him down. If he tried to argue that statement in any way, I was going to lay him out.

I must have been pretty obvious because the adults all chose that exact moment to intervene.

"Be back by twelve thirty."

"You haven't had dinner yet!"

"Take your cell phones!"

I sputtered as I tried to figure out what everyone just said. "We'll get some dinner while we're out, Kaitlin. And Dad, come on. It's New Year's Eve. One o'clock."

My dad rolled his eyes. "One," he agreed grudgingly. "But only because it's Avery, and I trust her to keep you out of trouble."

Normally I would argue that, but I just wanted to get poor Avery out of there. I grabbed her hand and whirled around toward the door. "Thanks, Dad!"

We'd almost escaped and then my mom said, "Grayson you come over here and give your mother a kiss goodbye before you go."

Suppressing a sigh, I grinned at my mom. "Last time I did that, you said it was bad manners."

The look she gave me said she wasn't in the mood, so I obeyed with no more arguments. "Thank you," she whispered as she brushed her lips on my cheek.

I pulled back and Kaitlin was right there, waiting for her turn to hug me. This was not a standard practice every time I left the house by any stretch. This was our moms, the worry twins, inwardly gushing over my rescuing Avery, so I wrapped my arms around Avery's mom and gave her an exaggerated bear hug. "Happy New Year, Kaitlin!"

She laughed when I gave her a big kiss on the cheek. "Always such a charmer, Grayson Kennedy."

I grinned. "Yes, ma'am."

"Just make sure you don't try to use that charm on my daughter tonight."

"Ms. Shaw!" I pretended to be scandalized. "I would never!"

Except apparently I would. I almost did upstairs not five minutes ago.

Kaitlin sobered up and lowered her voice so that only I could hear. "I mean it, Grayson. You be careful with her tonight. I'm sure she's really vulnerable right now."

Talk about a mood killer. I tried to sound sincere when I said, "She's practically a sister to me, Kaitlin. I'll behave myself."

This afternoon that statement would have been true. Now I just hoped I could get through the night without breaking my promise, because Kaitlin was right. Taking advantage of Avery right now would make me a bigger jerk than Aiden.

"You'd better," Kaitlin said, but there was teasing in her tone now.

"I will."

It was now or never. I grabbed Avery's hand again and made another break for the door. I even got it open this time, but Aiden just couldn't let us go. "Aves, are you really going to go out with *Grayson?*"

And I was back to being pissed off. I tried to keep walking, but Avery stopped. "Do you want me to stay with you?"

Balls! If he said yes, she would stay for him. Even after how much he hurt her today. And he *would* ask, the selfish punk. He's always gotten his way with her, ever since they were kids. He says jump, and she happily asks how high? It's not that he doesn't care about her. He just has the more dominant personality of the two, and apparently her feelings run a lot deeper than his, so she gives in to his every whim.

"Aves, of course I want you to stay. It's New Year's Eve, and we came here to spend it together."

Avery frowned. "But earlier you said—"

"I didn't mean I never wanted to see you again. You're still my best friend. You don't have to go out with him just to avoid me."

What the hell! I don't know what I ever did to him that

he thinks hanging out with me would be so awful. I'm an awesome big brother. "Maybe she wants to."

Aiden glared at me and then stomped over to us. "Do you, Avery? Do you actually want to go on a date with *Grayson?* Or are you doing this because of me?"

"I—" Avery's eyes darted frantically between Aiden and me and then they filled with tears.

"Aves," Aiden said in a voice that he had no right using on her. "Obviously I hurt your feelings earlier. I'm sorry. I was nervous, and I guess I didn't explain things right. Why don't you stay home tonight and we'll talk."

He reached up to wipe the tears from her face, and I almost decked him. I really wanted to, but I didn't have any claim to her. This was between the two of them as much as I didn't like it.

"Maybe that's a good idea," Kaitlin interrupted. "I think the two of you need to try and work this out."

I cringed. To have to go through all this with our freaking *parents* eating up every word like a trashy novel? I would hate to be Avery right then. I wanted to kill Aiden for putting her in this position!

Avery's grip on my hand loosened, but she didn't let go. She glanced around the room and then set those big, honest eyes on Aiden. "Do you love me?" she asked.

I choked on some spit.

"Aves, you're my best friend. You're practically my twin sister. Of course I love you."

He was clueless. The friggin' moron was completely clueless.

Avery's face paled and her hand started shaking in mine. I gave her a gentle squeeze just to let her know I was still there, and suddenly she clamped down on my hand so hard I almost cursed.

Her voice trembled as she whispered, "I love you too, Aiden." Then, still crushing the bones in my hand, she looked up at me. Her desperation was obvious. "You ready?"

I didn't miss a beat. "Hell yeah."

I dragged her out of there without letting her look back.

denial

Avery

If Grayson weren't propelling me forward with the arm he had around my shoulders, I would probably have still been standing on the front steps to the condo building. I was in shock all over again.

I couldn't believe it. I mean I *literally* could not believe it. As in, my brain physically wouldn't accept the information.

"He has to be wrong," I mumbled as Grayson strolled me down the street. "He didn't know what he was saying. He didn't understand what I was asking."

"He definitely didn't get it, but Aves…" Grayson sighed.

"He can't know whether or not he loves me if he's never given it a thought. I've been so patient, all these years. Maybe I just needed to say something. Maybe if I'd just kissed him once."

"I don't know, Avery. He's pretty dense, but a guy doesn't just ask for space if he's in love with you. Even if his love is subconscious."

I think this conversation was making Grayson uncomfortable, but I couldn't stop myself. My brain was stuck in a loop because moving forward meant acknowledging that Aiden saw me as a sister, and that was simply unacceptable.

"He just hasn't ever considered the possibility of a relationship between us," I insisted. "Maybe he hasn't hit that level of maturity yet. I mean it's not like he's ever gone out with anyone else. He never talks about any other girls."

"Maybe he's gay."

"Grayson!" He was laughing at his own joke. "Aiden is not gay! Don't you even joke about that! It's *not* funny."

"Come on, it's a little funny. It would also explain how he could spend almost seventeen years with a girl like you and never make a move, because no straight guy could do that."

My stomach did this weird flip. Had Grayson always been so sweet? I hadn't thought so, but he'd been incredible since the moment I jumped in his shower.

I leaned into him, sagging against his side, and the next thing I knew, my arms were around his waist and I was hugging him. He stopped walking and hugged me back. When his arms pulled me tight against him, all of the tension left

33

my body.

"I didn't realize you were so nice, Grayson."

The warm sound of Grayson's chuckle rumbled pleasantly against the side of my face that was resting on his chest. "Damsels in distress have always been my Achilles' heel, but don't let that fool you. I'm really not that nice."

"Yes, you are."

"No, I'm not. If I was nice, I wouldn't be having such a hard time not grabbing your butt right now."

I gasped and shoved away from him. He let me go but caught my hand and intertwined our fingers. His holding my hand made me blush even worse than his perverted comment had.

Since I couldn't bring myself to look at him, I didn't notice when he stopped walking until I was yanked to a halt. He stood in front of a small bistro with a questioning look. "Hungry? Dinner's on me tonight."

The restaurant was dark and cozy with soft lighting. Grayson helped me out of my coat, then held out my chair for me before taking his seat directly across from me at the small, candlelit table for two.

The moment was so surreal. I always knew Grayson was charming. There was a reason he'd dated most of the girls in school, and yet they still kept lining up to be his next fling.

Seeing Grayson Kennedy in action and being the focus of his attention were two entirely different things. He wasn't doing it on purpose to seduce me or anything, but even set on "friendly," he was freaking me out a little.

The server brought out glasses of ice water, and I started

chugging mine because Grayson was making me so nervous.

"You might want to slow down there, slugger, before you get a…" I winced and Grayson laughed. "… headache."

As Grayson watched me, his eyes sparkled in the dim light, making him look like he'd just stepped off the set of a Hollywood movie. Aside from his tall, broad frame and amazing body, Grayson Kennedy had the entire package where looks were concerned. He was Spanish Fork High's golden boy: hair the color of amber, eyes so blue they looked unreal, and golden skin that didn't have a single blemish, freckle, or scar.

His teeth were perfect, and he spent so much time smiling that the gesture on him was a work of art. He even had this one adorable dimple that only showed itself when he was really, truly happy about something. That dimple was present now.

I broke the silence with a nervous laugh. "This is awkward, isn't it?"

Grayson pursed his lips until they turned white because he was trying so hard not to laugh at me. "Awkward? What's awkward?"

He knew darn well what I was talking about! Grayson was always torturing me like that. I asked him why he did it once, and his answer had been because it was fun to make me blush. Well, mission accomplished, Mr. Kennedy. I was beet red. Again.

He was waiting for an answer.

"You know…" I squirmed in my chair. "This. Us. Being here like this."

Grayson suppressed another laugh. "Being here like what?"

"I don't know. This restaurant is so…atmospheric, and you helping me with my coat and pulling out my chair." I was now so red that my face was going to stain permanently. "It just feels, I don't know, sort of like…like a…"

"Like a date?" Grayson asked. He wasn't laughing anymore. He met my eyes with a startling intensity.

I couldn't find my voice, so I just nodded.

He gave me another heart-stopping smile. "That's because it is a date, Avery."

I felt my eyes grow to three times their normal size, but no matter how hard I tried, I couldn't get them to stop. "What?" I gasped. "No, it's not!"

"Yes, it is."

His voice left no room for argument, but that didn't stop me. "We can't be on a date!"

"Why?"

"Because you're…you're…you're you and I'm me! We grew up together! We're practically family!"

Grayson frowned—a real one, not his usual pout-to-get-his-way sad face. "You grew up with Aiden too."

All the air left my lungs. "That's different."

"How so?"

"Because he doesn't treat me like a sister."

Grayson looked like he was about to argue that, but I really didn't want to discuss Aiden, so I quickly said, "*You*, on the other hand, act like an annoying, gross older brother."

"Gross?" I thought he'd be offended, but he actually

laughed. "You think I'm *gross?*"

"Yes, I do. You are so horny it's unhealthy. You burp in my face every time you eat onions, and you don't bother to leave the room before you fart. This afternoon you dripped your sweat on me. On purpose!"

"Okay, okay. You've got me there. I will admit that our relationship has always had more of a sibling vibe. But the truth of the matter is that you gave me a total hard-on today and—"

"Oh my gosh, Grayson, shut up!" I shrieked in a whisper, burying my face in my hands. "Please don't ever, *ever* say something like that again!"

"You've got to face the facts, Aves. If you were really my sister and we'd ended up in the shower together, I'd have puked and hired a therapist. Not stared at your chest and wondered if you'd hit me if I took your shirt off."

"Oh my gosh!" My hands were starting to sweat because my face was so hot, but how was I supposed to remove them? That would require looking at Grayson, and there was no way I'd ever be able to do that again.

Grayson chuckled. "Aves, look at me."

"No! You were right. You are not nice! You are cruel!"

Grayson reached over the table and peeled my hands away from my flushed face. "I'm not being cruel," he said. I finally forced my eyes up to his.

He leaned his tall body over the tiny table so that he could look straight into my eyes. There was only a foot of space between us.

"This is most definitely a real date," he promised so

passionately it made me shiver. "I asked you out. I'm paying for your dinner. There *will* be dancing later, and I *will* be kissing you when the clock strikes twelve tonight."

I let out a tiny squeak of fear and Grayson upped his intensity. "It's going to happen, Aves, and you are going to like it."

Grayson's focus was interrupted by a small sigh. Thankfully! Because I'd stopped breathing again.

We both looked up to see our waitress standing over us, staring dreamily at Grayson. "Wow!" If she weren't holding our plates in her hands, she probably would have been fanning herself because she looked like she was about to melt. "And I thought my boyfriend was good." She smiled at me as she set my food in front of me. "Girl, you have got your hands full with this one, don't you?"

Grayson flashed her his biggest smile, and she winked at him as she left.

I'd never been so grateful to see a plate of food in my life—anything to give me an excuse not to look at him and stop this conversation.

Grayson must have seen that he'd pushed me to my limit, because he went to work on his dinner and let me eat in peace.

Unfortunately, the silence let my thoughts wander back to the reason I was out with Grayson in the first place. I set my fork down, unable to eat another bite.

Grayson set his fork down too. "Avery, I promised your mom you'd eat."

I could feel tears in my eyes when I looked up at him.

"Why you?" I asked. "Why are you the one here with me? Why isn't it him?"

Grayson's smile was sad and full of sympathy. "I don't know, Aves, but maybe it's for the best. You guys are almost seventeen. If it hasn't happened by now, maybe it's not supposed to."

"I can't accept that."

"Denial isn't good for you."

"It isn't denial."

"Now you're denying your denial."

"But look at you," I said. "You always thought I was like a sister too. If you can change your mind, then he can too. He just needs a wakeup call."

"Hey now, you can't just go jumping in the shower with every guy you know. That's totally *our* thing."

"Oh my gosh, Grayson, we do not have a thing!" The torture was never ending. "I wasn't talking about jumping in the shower with him," I mumbled. "But maybe if I just tell him how I feel, if I ask him to kiss me—to just give it a chance."

"And if he doesn't go for it?"

"He will. Grayson, I know he will. I know it here." I tapped my heart. "Aiden and I belong together. You'll see. He just needs to know how I feel. Maybe he believes I think of him like a brother and nothing else, you know? What if he's been in love with me for years, but he thinks I don't like him that way."

Grayson frowned and went back to his dinner. He obviously didn't agree, but I felt my excitement growing. "That's got to be it! It makes so much sense! What if he said he needed space because it hurts him to be with me but not *with* me? What if I'm hurting him? You saw how mad he got tonight when you said you were taking me out. He was jealous."

Now my excitement had been replaced with dread. I didn't want to hurt Aiden ever. But what else could all this have been about? Nothing else made any sense. "He asked me to talk, and I walked out on him! I'm awful!"

Grayson rolled his eyes. "You are not. He was a jerk. He deserved what you did. Worse even."

I shook my head. "Thank you for being so nice to me tonight and trying to help me. I'm sorry to ditch you, but I need to go home and talk to Aiden."

Grayson sat there as if he were giving the whole situation some serious thought. Eventually I saw acceptance wash over his face and he set down his fork. "I suppose you do need to talk to him, don't you. But if you do this, you can't hold anything back. You've got to give it to him straight. Tell him everything. Just be sure to use small words so he can understand."

"I will." I smiled for the first time all evening and jumped up to give Grayson a hug and a kiss on the cheek. "Thank you for understanding. You are the best big brother I've never had!"

Grayson let go a small laugh and shook his head. "Not your brother, Aves."

"You never know," I teased. "You could be someday."

He smiled again, but this time it didn't quite reach his

eyes "Good luck."

"Thanks."

I burst through the door to the condo less than five minutes later. The adults had cracked open the wine and were laughing a little loudly, but that stopped the instant they saw me.

For once the attention didn't paralyze me. Breathless from my run and excited to figure things out with Aiden, I hurried and threw my coat, hat, and scarf haphazardly onto the rack by the door. "Where's Aiden?"

"Up in the boys' room," Cheryl answered cautiously. "Where's Grayson?"

"If I had to guess? On his way to apartment 7B."

My mom's forehead creased, and she set down her glass of wine. "Did you guys have a fight?"

"Oh! No!" Realizing what they were all worried about, I gave them my most reassuring smile. "Grayson is the best! Who knew he could be so sensitive?" I remembered the comment about wanting to take my shirt off and cringed. "Well, sort of sensitive."

None of the parents seemed to know what to say.

"Grayson and I had a nice time," I assured them. "I just really need to talk to Aiden now."

I ran up the stairs without waiting for any responses.

I took a deep breath, and then knocked on Aiden's bedroom door. Thanks to this afternoon's shower debacle, I was pretty sure I'd never forget to knock ever again.

"Yeah?"

"Can I come in?"

A split second later the door flew open. Aiden was positively livid. "What happened? Did he make a move on you? I'll kill him!"

Aiden looked so funny when he was angry. His adorable face just wasn't meant to hold such negative emotions.

Aiden looked a lot like his brother, and yet he didn't. Aiden was a lot shorter, but he had the same coloring as Grayson—same rich golden hair and skin. He had brown eyes and not blue, but he and Grayson shared the same perfect smile. The difference, though, is where Grayson's smile labeled him as an obvious lady-killer, that same smile made Aiden look like the adorable class clown. Fury just didn't work well for him.

"I'm fine, Aiden." I laughed. "Grayson didn't make a move on me." Well, not technically. I didn't think. He hadn't yet, anyway.

"Then what's wrong?"

"Nothing's wrong. I just felt bad for walking out on you. You asked me to stay and talk, and you were right. We really need to."

Aiden sagged in relief and pulled me into a hug. "I'm really sorry, Aves. I totally screwed that up earlier. I didn't want to hurt your feelings."

I squeezed him back. It felt so good that I almost cried. For a while I thought I'd never feel this again. "It's okay. What happened was just as much my fault as yours. We should have talked about this years ago."

Aiden was surprised by my comment. I tugged him over to the bed with me, and we sat shoulder to shoulder.

He picked up my hand and rested his head on mine. "I don't ever want to lose you, Avery. I don't think I could handle that."

My heart, which had hurt so bad just minutes before, suddenly soared. "Me either." I took a breath. No time like the present. "I love you so much, Aiden."

"I know, Aves. Me too."

"No, I don't think you do know. I'm saying I'm *in love* with you."

Aiden's grip on my hand tightened. "What?"

"I'm in love with you, Aiden. I have been for years and years. I should have said something, but I always just figured you'd get it when you were ready."

I let out a huge breath. I couldn't believe it. After so long my deepest secret, my biggest frustration, was finally out there. Aiden finally understood.

"Oh no, Aves," Aiden said quietly. "No. No, don't say that."

"Wait! Hear me out." I swallowed back my sudden nerves. The devastation in his voice had shaken my confidence. "I get what you were trying to say earlier. I totally understand you needing some space and some things to do on your own. You want to go join the debate team, fine. That's great. I'll support you. You can go be you, and I can go be me, but we can do that and still be *us*. I know we need a change, but what I'm saying is that I want things to change in the romantic direction. I've *always* wanted that."

"Aves…" Aiden's voice broke, and his hand started shaking.

"I know that must sound crazy to you, but I'm sure it could work. I've never been so sure about anything in my life. You are it for me. I love you, and I want you to love me back."

Just then a tear splashed down onto the back of my hand that Aiden was holding in his lap. I glanced up and met his eyes, surprised to see the streak of moisture running down his face. I'd never seen Aiden cry before.

I didn't understand. He was so sad. It was as if somehow *I'd* just broken *his* heart.

"Avery, I am so sorry." His voice had a sort of helplessness to it. "I—I didn't know. You never said—you never acted like—I assumed it was the same for us. You're my best friend, but that's it. I don't think of you that way."

Moisture was gathering in my eyes now too. I blinked and a tear fell down my cheek. "How do you know if you've never given it a chance?" I squeezed his hand and mustered up every ounce of courage I had in me. "Will you kiss me, Aiden? Please? Just once? Maybe that's all you need. Maybe if we kissed, you'd feel what I feel."

Aiden closed his eyes. When he shook his head, it looked as if the action caused him pain. "I'm sorry, Aves, but I can't. I have a girlfriend now."

"You…"

Who knew a heart could break twice? This time it was so bad I didn't even feel it. I didn't feel anything. I actually stopped crying. It was like his confession just…broke me.

"Mindy Perez," Aiden whispered. "We were partners all semester in public speaking and…it just happened the last day of school."

Aiden had a girlfriend.

He'd left me high and dry without a science project partner, ditched me as co-president of science club, told me he needed space, bailed on me for our birthday next month, said he loved me like a twin sister, and I'd been so in denial that I actually thought I'd still stood a chance with him.

I was so stupid.

I believed it now. The second stage of grief was complete. Stage three too. I'd done enough bargaining. I'd asked him to love me, begged him to kiss me—to just give me a chance. It didn't work, and now I was done with that. I wouldn't do it again. Aiden Kennedy was never going to love me, and there was nothing I could do about it.

"Okay." I shook myself and rose to my feet.

"Aves!" He tried to keep hold of my hand, but I managed to slip out of his grip. "Avery, wait! I'm so sorry. Please don't be mad."

I stopped in the doorway and turned back to him. He was still sitting on his bed, looking every bit as upset as I felt.

"I'm not mad," I promised, and at the time, it was true. Someone who is completely dead inside can't be mad. They can't really be anything.

social integration

Grayson

I totally discovered something lamer than journals. Being stuck in a condo for two days with an idiot brother that you want to pound in the face, while he's acting all emo (As if he had any right to be depressed, the stupid jerk!), and Avery while she's having a full-on mental breakdown. Seriously. Break. Freaking. Down. The girl turned into a zombie, complete with the limited speech abilities and glazed over eyes.

Who'd have ever thought that I would actually be glad to start school again?

I was a little anxious to see Avery. I hadn't seen or heard from her since we left the condo. She wasn't answering her cell phone, and I wasn't allowed to call Kaitlin and ask. She and my mom were having the mother of all best friend fights because their children had broken each other's hearts and, of course, in both cases, it was the other woman's kid who was to blame for the "misunderstanding."

I sort of felt guilty about what happened. I shouldn't have sent Avery back to Aiden that night. I knew my brother. I knew Avery was going to get shot down, but she couldn't see it, or had refused to see it anyway. I figured his official rejection was not just inevitable but necessary, so I let her go.

I didn't know Aiden had a secret girlfriend bomb to drop on her. Avery would have found out soon enough anyway, and better she had a few days to cope in private instead of just being blindsided at school. But still, I couldn't help feeling like I hadn't protected her enough.

I sat in the cafeteria drumming my fingers on the lunch table like a crack addict suffering withdrawals as I watched the door for Avery. We'd never spoken at school before. We didn't have any classes together, and we were in *way* different social circles, so I hardly ever even saw her, but I knew we had the same lunch. I also knew that she sat with my brother every day. Except now that he and his new leash holder were public with their relationship, I didn't know what that meant for Avery.

I was scared for her, which was kind of a new feeling for me because I never really pay that much attention to anyone. Aves was just so destroyed after New Year's Eve that I couldn't help myself. I was either stepping up as the role of overprotective big brother, or I'd developed an impossible crush and was pissed off that someone dared hurt my woman. I had no idea which it was.

Turns out I was every bit as tangled up in our warped relationship as Avery and Aiden. Thanks a lot, moms. Prenatal yoga classes should be illegal.

"No!"

My worst fear was about to happen. Avery had just been dragged into the cafeteria by some fellow nerd girl. Aves was whiter than a sheet and shaking her head in protest, but her friend had a grim look of determination on her face and was dragging Avery toward their lunch table.

I was glad to see that at least one person from Aiden and Avery's little nerd herd had taken her side, but one girl wasn't going to be enough. Aiden's new girlfriend was a real piece of work. She'd come over to the house the day before and steamrolled her way to a place the family. She was loud, outspoken, and determined. She knew what she wanted and she meant business.

Unfortunately, what Mindy Perez wanted most was Avery out of Aiden's life completely. I'd overheard her telling him that keeping up a friendship with Aves was totally inappropriate. He'd tried to tell her that he didn't want to stop being friends with Avery, but the conversation still ended with him promising he'd "do something about it."

"No, no, no, no, no!"

There were only two open seats at Avery's table and one

was right next to Aiden. This was not going to be pretty.

"Yo Grayson! What's up with you, man?"

"Yeah, Gray, baby, what's wrong?"

"She'll eat her alive," I muttered, and then, suddenly, I was on my feet, ignoring my friends and crossing over into the unpopular side of the cafeteria.

I got there just in time to watch Avery's friend plunk her down in her usual seat at Aiden's side, then take the seat next to her and say to the whole table, "Hey guys! How was everyone's break? I got the new Celestron SkyProdigy 70 for Christmas! I'm going to have a stargazing party this weekend. You're all invited." She leaned around Avery to glare at Aiden. "Except for you."

I had to give the girl props for that one, even though I had no clue what a Celestron SkyProdigy 70 was.

A few people gave nervous replies, but then Mindy cleared her throat. It was the tiniest little sound, and yet it silenced the entire table. Aiden's shoulders hunched in response to it.

"Hey, um, Aves?" Aiden asked.

Mindy elbowed him, and he corrected his use of our nickname for Avery.

"I mean Avery? Um, do you think you could…um…I mean, would you mind—ow, ow, ow, ow!"

I'd grabbed his ear and yanked him back hard. "You utter one more word of that sentence, little brother, and I will kick your ass into next Tuesday."

I had everyone's attention, and I don't just mean the dorks at Avery's table.

I don't know that I'd ever sounded more menacing, but I don't think I'd ever been more out of my mind with rage either. The little pissant was about to ask Avery to leave her own lunch table and not sit by him anymore in front of all of her friends.

Aiden wisely hadn't said another word, and all his friends were staring up at me completely terrified, except for Mindy. She just sort of blinked at me in disbelief. I'm pretty sure she'd assumed my family all loved her simply because she'd expected it of us.

"Aves, get up."

"Huh?"

I had to work to control the anger in my voice. "Get up," I repeated. "You are not sitting here anymore."

Avery shook herself out of a daze and then scrambled obediently to her feet.

"Aiden, grow some balls you whipped bastard." I let go of his ear with a little push, snapping him back into his seat. Then I glared at the girl next to him. "Mindy." She paled when I spoke her name. "Avery is a hundred times the person you will ever be. If you say a single unkind thing to her or about her to anyone *ever*, you will be socially crucified. Get me? I will make it my personal mission in life to ruin you."

She stared up at me in disbelief, but she looked scared. She should. I wasn't kidding, and she seemed like the kind of person who cared very much about her reputation.

Next, I pointed a finger at Avery's chubby little friend who'd dragged her to her table. "And you…" The girl flinched and looked like she was about to vomit. I felt bad because I hadn't meant to scare her. "You seem pretty cool. Thanks for looking out for my girl. Keep up the good work."

With that, I grabbed Avery's hand and dragged her back toward my table on the other side of the cafeteria.

"Grayson!" Avery pleaded in a shocked whisper. "What are you doing?"

"You deserve better than that, Aves. You eat lunch with me from now on, okay?"

"Um…" She was still trying to put on the breaks. "That is really sweet of you and all, Grayson, but I don't know. I mean I don't exactly fit in with your friends. I'm…I'm…"

"You're *what?*" Her insecurity was frustrating. She was worth more than she thought of herself. She needed to understand that.

She gulped. "Well, you know, I'm not popular."

I stopped only because she was terrified and about to have another panic attack. "Aves, you'll be fine. My friends will be cool. You'll see."

"I don't know. I think I've seen this movie, and it doesn't turn out so well for me."

I smiled at that, even though she hadn't meant it to be funny. "How much you want to bet? I'm sure you've seen nature shows on alpha males or pack leaders or whatever— the whole flock of sheep thing, right?" I turned my smile extra confident because I know it annoys her when I act cocky. "Aves, Grayson Kennedy is at the top of the Span- ish Fork High food chain. I'm the king of the jungle. My friends will like you because I like you."

She didn't look entirely convinced, but she wasn't going to hyperventilate anymore, either.

"You're all about experiments and stuff," I said. "So let's do an experiment. Come eat lunch with me, at least for today, and let me introduce you to my friends. We will put *Animal Planet* to the test, and if I can't have all of my friends completely enamored with you by the end of lunch, then I'll back off and you can take your one cool friend and go hide out in the science lab every lunch for the rest of the year." Geez, that sounded awful. I really hoped she didn't do that. "Come on, what do you say?"

She gazed up at me, and in her current post-trauma daze said the last thing I ever expected. "I'm surprised you know a word like enamored."

I burst out laughing and wrapped my arm around her shoulders. "Yeah, three syllables is pretty much my limit."

Avery didn't protest anymore as I dragged her over to my friends, but she started to panic when we reached the table. I suppose I couldn't blame her, considering my friends were all sitting there gaping at me as if I'd lost my mind and was introducing them to a piece of scum I got on my shoe while I was over in no-man's land.

"Guys, this is Avery," I said conversationally. "Everybody shove down and make some room for her." I paused and gave Avery a grin, hoping to break some of the tension. "Unless you want to sit on my lap?"

I'm sure deep inside her somewhere she knew I was only teasing her, but she looked at me with eyes as big as baseballs and frantically shook her head. Her stupid panic was taking over.

I knew this might be an issue. Avery's anxiety was legitimate. She was diagnosed with social anxiety disorder a few years back. She even took medication for it. The drugs allowed her to come to school—they'd talked about homeschooling her when she hit middle school and started having too many problems—but even the medicine couldn't fix everything.

Avery didn't handle change well, and meeting strangers was almost impossible. That my friends were all seniors and the most popular kids in school had to be making this scarier for her too. Then there was the fact that we were both the main focus of everyone in the cafeteria right now because I'd caused a scene. I kicked myself for that one, but it was too late now. I couldn't undo it, so instead I tried to help her come back from freak-out mode.

She seemed to do better when all she could see was my eyes, so I grabbed her cheeks and pulled her face close to mine. "Remember what we talked about with the whole breathing thing? You've got to do it, Aves." I prompted her by taking a deep breath, and eventually she copied the action. After a few more I smiled at her. "You good now?" It was the same thing I'd asked her in the shower, and I think we were both remembering that, because her cheeks turned pink as she nodded.

I sat her down at the table next to me and tucked her safely into my side. She shook a little as she clung to me, but she didn't lose it. I was proud of her for regaining control of herself. For a second there I didn't think she was going to make it.

I was going to have to be very careful about this transition, but there was no way I could leave her to deal with Aiden and Mindy on her own. That would get her pulled from school in a matter of days.

"Well done, Aves," I whispered as I planted a kiss on the side of her head. "Hardest part's over now."

I stuck a tater tot in front of her face until she rolled her eyes at me and ate it. Not that I was a fan of feeding people or anything, I was just stalling as I figured out the best way to proceed with my friends.

"Have you really been through so many girls at this school that you're stealing them from the geeks now?" my best friend Owen Jackson teased.

"Nah, Avery's cool. We've been like this"—I crossed my fingers—"since before she was born. Really. I used to read picture books to her while she was still in her mom's stomach."

A couple of the girls gave us pouty little "Awws," and I knew we would be fine. The guys would be a little trickier, but nothing I couldn't handle.

"Didn't I just take her picture for the *science club* before break?"

I cringed inwardly. That was the one thing my friends might not be able to swallow about Avery. I'd been hoping they wouldn't realize that until they knew her better. I'd forgotten that Mark was the photographer for the yearbook staff.

I plastered a wicked smile on my face and said, "Well,

yes, but we're going to forgive her that one nerdy offense because Avery looks really hot in the shower."

Avery choked on the food in her mouth and started coughing. I hoped I hadn't just stopped her heart permanently, but I needed the guys to see her as dating potential and science club president was pretty much the opposite of that.

"No way, dude! You guys *showered* together?"

"It was the highlight of my winter break."

"Grayson!" Aves finally shrieked. "Shut up! We did not shower together!"

"We most certainly did. Were we not in the shower at the same time?"

"That's not the same thing!"

"Was there not nakedness involved?"

She slapped her hands over her flaming face, completely mortified. I squeezed her to me even tighter, praying she'd forgive me eventually. I'd reached her limit and needed to pull back, but that was okay because every guy at that table was now looking at her differently. In fact, maybe I'd done too good of a job because some of their looks were starting to piss me off.

I sighed, trying to sound repentant and yet not at the same time. "All right, so we didn't actually *shower* together. My jerk-off little brother, who's been her best friend for nearly *seventeen years,* bailed on her out of the blue for Mindy the Psycho Perez. Our moms were going crazy, so Avery jumped in the shower to hide from them. I just happened to be in there at the time. Aves was fully clothed, sadly, and had her eyes closed the whole time, so she missed out on seeing all my good stuff. I swear her honor and virtue are both still fully in tact. Much to my dismay."

I got a few snickers from my friends, and a groan from Avery, who still wouldn't pull her face out of her hands.

"I covered for her, we had a moment, she looked amazing in a wet t-shirt, it was super hot, and yes, Aves, it was the highlight of my winter break. Until later that night when you let me take you out on a date, and then *that* was the highlight of my winter break."

"Aw, you guys are dating now? That's so cute!"

I smiled really big at my friend Pamela. She was the queen bee of the girls in this school, and the only one I really needed to like Avery. If I could win her over, Aves would be set. She was watching Avery and me with a dreamy smile—a very good sign.

"Not exclusively," I said. "Aves is still free to play the field if she wants, but we're definitely feeling out the possibility."

I was anyway. I hadn't been able to stop thinking about her since New Year's Eve. We needed to go out again and finish the date we'd started. The girl owed me a kiss.

"Oh my gosh, *Grayson*, we are *not* dating!"

So she still considered me the gross older brother. At least she was showing her face again. If you ask me, her social integration was going rather well.

"I thought we were past the denial," I teased her. "Shouldn't you be at acceptance now? Isn't that what comes after denial?" Everyone frowned at me now. "You know, like when somebody dies?" I explained. "There are those stages…"

"Yeah, yeah, yeah!" Owen snapped his fingers a number of times while he tried to figure out a way to explain. "You start out in denial, and then you get all depressed, and finally you learn to accept the truth."

I looked down at Avery and smiled. "Well you were definitely depressed all weekend, so we should be good now, right? Acceptance? You want to go out this Friday? Maybe not ditch me halfway through dinner this time?"

I gave Avery the grin that I know she can't stay mad at, and sure enough, she pursed her lips together like she was trying not to smile. "I was depressed about *Aiden*, not you, and I am nowhere close to reaching any sort of acceptance over that."

"Oh, that's because you have to get angry first," Pamela said. "That's one of those stages too." She glanced across the cafeteria and scowled my brother's direction. "Shouldn't be too hard to do. I can't believe he dumped you for that Mindy girl. I had trig with her last year. She is *so* awful. You know what? I'll help you get angry, and then you can move on to acceptance and go out with Grayson because you're so tiny and he's so tall. It would completely adorable."

Avery blushed, and even I had to fight back a small tightness in my chest.

"So true!" Pamela's best friend Chloe agreed. "About your cuteness and about Mindy. She's the worst. But you don't need to get angry, you need to get even. Is that one of those stages?"

"I don't think so," Avery whispered shyly. She was actually talking to them now! Very, very good sign.

"Well it should be, because the key to curing a broken heart is not anger. It's revenge." She suddenly reached across the table and grabbed one of Avery's hands. "Do you want to come over to my house today after school? Pam and I are awesome with makeovers. We can shake you up a bit and make you so desirable that Aiden will kick himself until he dies for dumping you."

"Oh, it would be so easy!" Pam agreed. "You're totally adorable already, and with you dating Grayson? Wow. That is going to drive Aiden crazy!"

"Ooh!" Chloe squealed. "The best part about it all is that Aiden going crazy about Avery will drive Mindy absolutely insane with jealousy!"

Owen leaned close to me and muttered, "Dude. Girls are crazy."

I had to agree, but inside I was getting really excited. This was exactly what I was hoping would happen. Pam and Chloe would be the perfect people to take Avery under their wings. They could show her all that girl stuff that I couldn't help her with.

"Um." Avery shrunk a little closer to me, but I gave her a nudge, forcing her to sit up on her own. "That is so nice of you guys, but I don't need revenge. I don't want to hurt Aiden's feelings."

I suppressed an eye roll. Obviously she hadn't hit anger yet.

Aves tipped her head up to look at me and grimaced.

"We *aren't* dating. I just got my heart broken. I'm not really ready to date anyone, and, I'm sorry, I'm definitely not in the mood to be your flavor of the weekend."

I chuckled and so did most everyone else. It wasn't every day that I got shot down. It was kind of amusing. "I believe the term is flavor of the week," I teased. "Not weekend."

Avery looked at me skeptically. "Have you ever lasted an entire week with one girl?"

For a single beat there was silence, and then the entire table exploded into laughter. Everyone razzed me like crazy over the burn. The beauty of it was that Avery had been completely serious. Her innocence was genius.

Avery blushed of course, but I sat up a little straighter. I felt a strange fluttering of pride in my stomach. Avery had won them over! This was going to work. The first step to helping Avery Shaw was a complete success.

social science

Avery

Despite my claims to Grayson that loving to learn didn't make me a dork, the truth is, I knew I was a geek. I didn't mind, though. I really did enjoy learning, and I spent my entire life in the blissful world of social obscurity. Grayson Kennedy changed all that in the span of a single lunch period.

Suddenly I was the subject of many rumors—the most popular being that I was Grayson's new girlfriend. Everyone in school knew my name. People who'd never spoken to me before acted like we were best friends. It was crazy. Not that

I didn't appreciate what Grayson had done, but I wasn't sure if he'd made things better for me, or worse.

I missed all of fifth period because I had to go to the nurse to take one of my pills that they keep on hand for when I can't control my panic attacks. That led to my guidance counselor asking questions as to why I was having such bad anxiety. I threw her for a loop with the unprecedented change in social status. I guess that kind of thing didn't happen a lot in high school.

The only truly relieving thing that came from all the madness was that Grayson and his friends had given me an idea for a science fair project—a project that I technically already had a decent start on, so even without a partner, I had a good chance of getting it done on time. By the time school was over that day, I had a full outline of my project scribbled down to show Mr. Walden in science club.

I'd been so busy putting my project outline together that I managed to block out all the whispers and stares. I hardly noticed when Aiden changed seats and completely ignored me in Honors English. Okay, I noticed, and it killed me, but thanks to the outline (and the very powerful medication), I'd been able to live through it and not have another breakdown.

I was the last one to arrive in the science lab after school because Grayson's friends Pamela and Chloe found me and tried to convince me to go with them to Chloe's for a makeover. I said I had science club, but they wouldn't leave until I'd promised to go with them the next day.

When I got to the science lab, Libby, my friend who'd

been with me at lunch when Grayson hijacked me, tackled me. Since I'd missed fifth period, we hadn't seen each other yet. "Oh my heck, Avery!"

Libby was my best, and only, girl friend. She was brilliant and nice and very spunky. She was very outgoing and so funny that anyone who gave her a chance loved her; but because she wasn't as thin as the majority of girls in our school and had a tendency to wear pictures of cats on her clothes, most people didn't give her a chance. Most people were shallow idiots.

She threw her arms around me and forced me to jump up and down with her. "Can you believe that happened?"

"What exactly are we talking about? Aiden getting a girlfriend? Or Grayson almost killing him in front of the whole school?"

"I'm talking about how your romantic, hot new boyfriend came to your rescue in front of everyone! Seriously, Avery. Didn't you just *die?*"

I flushed at her phrasing. "Grayson's not my boyfriend, and yes, I did almost die, actually. That's why I missed calculus today. I had to go take a pill and have a major freak out in the guidance office."

"Seriously, Aves? You had to go to the office?"

Libby looked over my shoulder at the new voice. I didn't need her bugged-out eyes and squeak of excitement to tell me who was behind me sounding so concerned.

Before I could ask Grayson what he was doing at science club, he grabbed me by the shoulders and looked me over as if searching for signs of distress. "You okay?"

"Yes. I keep special medication in the nurse's office for emergencies, so I'm okay now."

Grayson's face fell. "You had an episode?"

"It wasn't too bad. There were just so many people staring and whispering after lunch."

"I'm sorry. That was all my fault." Grayson crushed me to his chest. "I knew I shouldn't have made a scene like that, but Aiden was being such a jerk, and I totally lost my temper. Forgive me?"

I carefully untangled myself from Grayson's grip. My face was flaming from his attention. I knew all of science club was watching us. That may have only been four other people besides me, but they were pretty much the only four friends I had. I was sure they thought I was crazy by now.

"What are you doing here?" I finally asked.

Grayson shrugged. "Detention," he said and then smirked. "Got a lot of texts after lunch today. Did you know that you're my girlfriend?"

I ignored that comment and said, "You're taking Mr. Walden's class?"

"Failing his class, actually,"

"Failing!"

Grayson gave me a sheepish smile. "Physics isn't my best subject. Bombed the final."

"Bombed is a good word for it," Mr. Walden said, walking into the room with a fresh mug of coffee.

"Do your parents know?" I asked.

"Yeah. They got the report card right before break. That wasn't so bad. It's Coach that was pissed. I'm benched until I can get my grade up."

"You can't play basketball? But you're a senior. If you don't play the rest of this season will you still be eligible to play for Utah Valley next year?"

"School policy." Grayson ran a hand through his hair like he was really stressed out but then looked at me, startled. "How'd you know I want to go to UVU next year?"

I rolled my eyes. "I've practically lived at your house my entire life. I know where you want to go to college."

"I have no idea where you want to go to college," Grayson said, frowning.

"That's not very surprising."

Grayson's frown grew even bigger. "Where do you want to go to college?"

"I'll tell you if you agree to let me help you with your physics grade."

"You mean like tutoring?"

"Sort of." It was my turn to smile at him for a change. I'd just gotten the most brilliant idea. I looked over at Mr. Walden, who was watching us from his desk with a surly expression. I suspect the only reason he didn't have Grayson doing extra homework yet was that Grayson was talking to me, and Mr. Walden loved me.

"Hey, Mr. Walden?"

Mr. Walden's eyes narrowed, but he must have been listening to our conversation, because he looked very curious. "Is it important, Avery? Science club is waiting for you, and Mr. Kennedy has a date with some trigonometric functions."

Grayson winced, and I had to bite my lip to keep from laughing at him.

"I assume Aiden spoke to you about quitting science club?"

Mr. Walden sighed. "He did. It's a real shame."

"Did he tell you that he wouldn't be doing the science fair with me, either?"

"Aiden wouldn't be so irresponsible as to quit on you with such short notice. Everyone else is already paired."

I pushed back the urge to cry again. "I'm on my own."

"That is so disappointing. I'm sorry. I'll have to speak with him."

"That's okay, Mr. Walden. I do have a project in mind, and I was just wondering…well, I need a partner, and Grayson could use some extra credit."

Mr. Walden blinked. So did Grayson. "You want me to do a *science project* with you?"

Grayson sounded comically horrified, but even more hilarious was the disbelief in Mr. Walden's tone. "You want *Grayson* to be your partner?"

I gave them both a look. "You haven't heard the project yet. It was Grayson's idea to begin with."

"Mine?" Grayson sounded startled.

"Yes, yours. And you're already doing it anyway. Sort of. Remember your experiment in the cafeteria this afternoon? My project is sort of like that." I handed Mr. Walden my outline. "I'm going to prove that the cure for a broken heart lies in the seven stages of grief."

As Mr. Walden read over my outline, Grayson looked

at me skeptically.

"Actually, Avery," Mr. Walden sounded impressed, "this is a very intriguing project. Very sound. The judges will really love the personal element too."

"I know the project isn't technically physics—I'll help him study that too, of course, to bring up his grade in class—but if he did the science fair with me, could it earn him enough extra credit to get him playing again? The team needs him, and it's his senior year. It would be awful for him to miss out."

Mr. Walden thought it over and then sighed. "I suppose as long as you were turning in weekly progress reports, I could talk to Coach Safford."

Grayson gasped. "For real, Mr. Walden? I can play? I don't have to miss any games?"

The look on Grayson's face told me he didn't usually have teachers willing to help him out. Sometimes it paid to be a nerd. I'd have to point that out to him later.

"If you do the work."

Grayson scooped me up into his arms and spun me in circles. He's so tall that my feet were at least a foot off the floor. "Holy shit, Aves! You're the best! I totally owe you forever!"

"Language, Mr. Kennedy," Mr. Walden scolded, but I noticed him bite back a grin when Grayson wasn't looking. He watched us for a moment longer and then said, "Actually, I believe you might be on to something with Grayson, Avery. The, uh, social aspect of this experiment is undeniably in his field of expertise. I believe he could do well with this project."

I laughed. Yes, Grayson would be the perfect partner.

Grayson put me down and eyed Mr. Walden and me warily. "Okay, what? I'm scared now. What in the world are you talking about? There is no way I am an expert in any form of science."

"Not physics, chemistry, or biology maybe."

"Actually, now that you mention it, I do all right with biology, if you know what I mean."

"Mr. Kennedy," Mr. Walden warned in a tired voice. "Avery, are you sure you want him for a partner?"

I laughed again. "I'm sure. Grayson was born for social science."

"Social science?" Grayson asked. "What is that?"

"I'll explain everything if you agree to be my science fair partner."

Grayson looked positively torn. I think he wanted to help me, and he knew he needed the extra credit, but he also looked like doing a science project might actually be the death of him.

"What would I have to do?" he asked. The question seemed to cause him physical pain.

"Nothing too awful. No equations, anyway. Since I'm going to be the test subject, all you have to do is help me through the seven stages of grief. I need an impartial perspective, and you've already helped me get past the shock and denial stages. I managed the bargaining on my own.

Sadly, it was rather pathetic, but then if you hadn't encouraged me to lay it all out to Aiden, I probably wouldn't have done that, either. So, really, you've helped me through them all so far. Now all you have to do is help me through the rest. Help me past my guilt and then the anger. Cheer me up when I get depressed, and finally, walk me through acceptance."

Grayson stared at me, dumbfounded. "You're saying that you want me to take you out and help you get over Aiden in any way I deem necessary—"

"I don't think I ever said *that*."

"Nope. I'm the unbiased opinion, remember? If we do this, you have to do what I say."

"Within reason," I argued.

"Within reason," Grayson agreed. "I make you forget my brother ever existed by taking you out on lots of really fun dates, and I get *extra credit* for that?"

"You'd have to keep a journal of it all. We'd have to catalog our experiments, compile our findings into an organized study, but yes. Basically."

Grayson still looked skeptical. "And that's considered *science?*"

I nodded. "Social Science. It's the study of people and relationships."

Grayson's jaw fell open. He blinked a few times and then let out an incredulous laugh. "You've got to be shitting me!"

"Mr. Kennedy, you're already in detention!" Mr. Walden released an exasperated sigh.

"Sorry. It's just, that actually sounds fun." Grayson looked at me, still in a bit of shock. "You've got yourself a deal, Aves. Consider me your science partner."

Mr. Walden clapped with satisfaction. "Great! It's settled then. Welcome to science club, Grayson."

"Wait, what?"

Mr. Walden chuckled. "That's my part of the deal. You want the extra credit, you take your brother's place in the science club. You come to the meetings, work on your project with Avery, and you attend the actual science fair with the team in March."

"You're not serious, Mr. Walden. Join the freaking science club? That's social *suicide*, not social science!"

"I am deadly serious. This is very important to Avery and the others. I will not let you take advantage of Avery's work ethics. You will pull your weight and be a part of the team, or you can sign up for after school tutoring and hope you get your grade up before the end of the season."

"Grayson, just say yes," I begged. "We've already taken our photo for the yearbook. I'll swear the gang to secrecy. No one will ever have to know."

Grayson gaped at my friends, who'd been hanging on every word of our conversation and were all staring back at him in just as much shock.

"Please?" I whispered, taking his hand. "Do this for me?"

Grayson took one look at my desperate, pleading face and gave in.

I threw my arms around his neck and kissed his cheek

as I squealed my thanks.

"And you said I'm cruel." He shook his head as I stepped back. "All I ever do is tease you. You just turned me into a dork."

life after aiden

Grayson

Okay, we will not discuss the fact that I am now an official member of the science club. I mean it. I almost said no to the entire deal because of the science club thing. Seriously, I think I'd rather fail physics and get kicked off the basketball team. But then Avery was there, hitting me full force with those big, hopeful eyes, and I couldn't let her down.

She doesn't understand the power she has with those beauties. I just joined the freaking science club for her! She thinks I did it for the extra credit, but I didn't. I would have done the tutoring and begged to retake my final or something. It was all for her. What was wrong with me?

After school the next day—that first official day of the Avery Shaw Experiment—Avery survived a girls-only trip to the mall with Pamela and Chloe and got a complete makeover. She debuted the look that night when Pam and Chloe dragged her to my basketball game. I saw them walk in the gym ten minutes after the game started and promptly tripped over my own feet, losing us the ball.

The tight shirt and short skirt were majorly distracting—in the best way possible—and the strawberry highlights were totally inspired. I'd never seen the girl look more amazing. She turned all kinds of heads that night and didn't even realize it.

I smiled to myself every time I overheard someone ask who the new hottie with Pam and Chloe was. Then I laughed when someone would answer that she was Grayson Kennedy's new girlfriend.

The rest of the week Avery tutored me after practice. Then I forced her to do something fun and exciting and out of her comfort zone that would help her forget about Aiden. We did things that she and Aiden never did, went places they never hung out, and I introduced her to people he didn't know.

She started referring to our time together as Life After Aiden. I called it Post Shower Avery and Grayson. She usually got mad at me for that. Usually. I considered the times she didn't bother to yell at me a small victory.

One week turned into two and all of the sudden I was completely turned upside down. Avery had given me free reign of her social life, so I was supposed to be in control, but when it came down to it, I wasn't in control of anything. Every choice I made was for her or about her. All of my free time was spent with her. It was like I was suddenly in a serious, steady, exclusive relationship but without any of the sexy benefits of a girlfriend. Crazy part was, I didn't seem to mind. Well, I minded the no-kissing part a little bit. That was getting harder and harder not to do.

Finding new things to make her try was an addictive game. She was just so adorable when she was experiencing something for the first time. She viewed everything so analytically at first, and she was always terrified, but then once she got past her anxiety, she would get so excited. It killed me every time.

On Friday night, the second week of the Avery Shaw Experiment and our first official date—meaning she'd given in and let me actually call it a date—I had the ultimate Post Shower Avery test planned. Tonight we would see just how much a new look and a few new friends had helped her.

"A *party?*"

I waited until I had her locked in my car to tell her where we were going, because I knew she was going to freak.

"A *college* party?"

Actually, her mom probably would have freaked too. And mine.

"It's not as bad as it sounds. A few friends of mine who graduated last year went in together on a house, and they're having some friends over."

"So it's a party."

"Yeah." I laughed. "It's a party. And most likely, it will be a little bit like the ones you see in the movies. I'm sure there will be lots of people drinking and making out, but I'm promising you right now that you don't have to do either of those things, and, for you, I will not partake of such activities either."

Come to think of it, this was going to be a new experience for me too. We'd see if a party was even still fun when you couldn't get drunk or make out with hot girls.

"Grayson, I know I said you could pick what we do, but I don't think I can do this one."

"Yes, you can. I'll be right by your side all night. It'll be an adventure. And if you really truly can't deal, then we can leave. Owen is taking Pam and Chloe in his car just in case this is a bust and we have to go early."

Avery glanced up hopefully, so I smiled a huge silly smile, showing off all my teeth. "See? I already planned on the possibility of it being too much for you."

Avery's knuckles, as she gripped the sides of her seat, got a little less white.

I reached over and patted her hand. "Aves, you have to trust me a little. The point is to push you out of you comfort zone, but I know you, okay? I won't overdo it. And I trust you too. If you say it's too much, then it's too much, and we'll leave. But just give it a try first, please?"

Avery stared out the front window in silence. After a minute she nodded her head. I think it was more to convince herself than it was an actual answer to my question.

When we pulled up to the house, the party was already

in full swing. Dozens of cars lined the street, and you could hear the music blasting from a block away. People spilled out of the house onto the front lawn, falling all over themselves in fits of laughter.

I had to drag Avery from the car. When she finally started walking, she stumbled. "Is it the heels?" I asked, pulling her to my side. "I don't think I've ever seen you wear high heels before, but they look hot. Plus it's kind of nice having you at shoulder height for a change instead of all the way down at my chest, shorty."

"Ha, ha," she said, but there was only nervousness in her voice. "It's not the heels. I practiced walking in them for over an hour. I'm just shaking too hard to walk."

I pulled her tight against me and kissed her temple. Her hair smelled fruity. She was one of those girls who always smelled good enough to eat. It drove me crazy.

"You'll be fine. Just hang on to me. I won't make you let go all night if you don't want to."

She took me up on my offer. Slowly, she slipped her arm around my waist and then clung to me like she was super glued there. I tensed beneath her touch and had to fight back shivers.

"Feel free to hang on to other parts of me too." My voice came out thick because it had been stuck in my throat. "My butt's feeling pretty left out, and I don't spend so much time working out my abs and chest just to never get felt up."

I laughed when Avery gasped and turned as red as the dress she had on. The super-hot, super-tight, amazing spaghetti-strap pencil dress that she'd been instructed to borrow tonight. Thanks to Chloe's petite Asian frame, Avery fit quite nicely into Chloe's clothes. Avery's ample chest was the only exception, and as a result, she was struggling to stay in the top of the dress. Thank you, Chloe!

My hand fell from Avery's shoulder down to the small of her back. It itched to go lower, but, miracle of miracles, it managed to stay put.

"Oh my gosh, Grayson! For once, could you please restrain from embarrassing me when I'm already on the verge of a massive freak out?"

"I was just putting the idea out there. I don't know if you're aware of how incredibly beautiful you look tonight, or that I haven't had a single hookup since The Shower Incident. That was *weeks* ago, Aves. I only have so much restraint."

Instead of smacking me or burying her face in her hands like I expected her to, Avery stopped walking and sighed. "You're right. This experiment has completely commandeered your life. I'm sorry. If you need to…" She hesitated, turning all pink again. "If you need to go do your thing or take care of business or whatever, I'll be okay with Pamela and Chloe for a while."

I felt a dopy smile creep over my face. I was on a role with that lately. There was no denying I was crushing on the girl now, but it was starting to get ridiculous. I was turning into some kind of freaking lovesick pansy, grinning every time I made the girl blush.

"You're giving me permission to go find a hot girl and hook up? On our first real date?"

"We can call the next one a date. You can have the night off tonight. You've earned it. Go have some fun. Find a gorgeous girl, act like yourself for five whole minutes until you've captured her heart, and then take her someplace quiet where you guys can *talk* for the rest of the night."

I had to bite the inside of my cheek through that speech to keep from smiling too much. "And what if I've already got my sights set on a gorgeous girl?"

She rolled her eyes, completely missing my meaning. "You're Grayson Kennedy. I'm sure you've already got your sights set on three or four different girls, and we aren't even in the front door yet."

Her comment stung. She hadn't meant it to be mean, and honestly, I totally deserved it, but things were changing for me, and I didn't like that I was the only one noticing. That moment was the first time I realized that I really, really liked Avery, and that I wanted her to like me too. For real like me.

"Aves, I was talking about you. You're my date tonight. I'm here with you because I want to be, okay? I don't need to go find anyone else. I may still need to hook up, though," I teased.

Avery frowned. "I don't understand."

Her naïveté was cute and frustrating at the same time. "That's because you don't see yourself the way I see you, but I'm going to fix that if I can."

I started walking us toward the house again, giving her time to let my words sink in, but the moment we stepped inside, all thought flew from Avery's mind. She froze, taking in the sight like a deer caught in the beams of a giant semitruck. The place was loud, chaotic, and packed—basically the opposite of everything Avery Shaw needed.

"Let's get something to drink and then see if we can find Owen and the girls," I shouted over the noise.

Avery turned around, buried her face in my chest, and held me like I was a life preserver. She squeezed me so tight I could barely breathe. I rubbed her back until I felt her take a breath.

After another look around the room, I sighed. I'd expected it to be a little crazy but not quite this much of a rager. This party was about as far from Avery's comfort zone as you could get. I figured she had about ten minutes in her. Tops.

We were still standing there like that when Owen and the girls found us. "This is wild, isn't it?" Owen asked slapping me a five.

"Is she okay?" Pamela asked, placing a hand on Avery's shoulder.

"I didn't think it'd be quite like this. Aves is having a little trouble with her anxiety. We might have to get out of here."

Both Pamela and Chloe looked disappointed. They'd really taken a liking to Avery. They treated her a little like a pet, but it worked well for all three of them. Pam and Chloe knew all about Avery's experiment—not that I was part of it or that I'd had to join the science club, but they knew Avery was doing this all for the science fair, and that I was trying to help. They loved the idea of a Get-Over-Aiden crusade and had instantly appointed themselves my co-assistant captains on Team Avery.

"Let's take her down to the basement for a minute before you give up. The DJ and the kegs are up here. They've still got the music playing downstairs, but it's not as crowded."

I dipped my head down to Avery's ear. "What do you think, Aves? Give it a try, or should we jet?"

Avery took a deep breath and then turned her head to the side so that I could hear her. It brought her face just inches from mine. If I tilted her head up the tiniest bit our lips would meet.

I kicked myself. The girl was fighting a panic attack. It wasn't exactly the time to be fantasizing about her hot sweet mouth on mine...or nibbling those soft pink lips...our tongues dancing...maybe I'd taste the freckles on her beautifully bare shoulder.

"I promised I'd give it a try." The quiver in her voice snapped me out of my daydream. "If Pamela says it's better downstairs, let's at least go see."

There is a God. It was much calmer downstairs. The lights were dim, the music was a little quieter, and there was plenty of room to breathe. It was a close call, but we didn't have to leave the party. After a while Avery even settled down enough that she sent me over to play a game of pool with Owen, while she chatted on a sofa with Pam and Chloe.

"Dude," Owen said after he'd missed his shot and I failed to notice it was my turn. "She's only five feet away.

You've got to relax a little."

"Yeah, no, I'm relaxed. I know she's fine." I took a deep breath and stretched. "It's just that dress…" I turned back around and focused on the pool table. "Two in the corner pocket."

"She does look good tonight," Owen admitted. "Makes me want to go check out the rest of the nerds at school, see who else is hiding out in the science lab."

I laughed. "Seven. Side pocket."

I missed my shot and immediately my eyes drifted back to Avery. She looked up, smiled, gave me a thumbs-up, and then laughed at something Pam said.

"I never thought I'd see the day Grayson Kennedy was off the market, but you, bro, are a player no longer." Owen sidled up next to me and joined me in watching the girls. Chloe was trying to get Pam and Avery to dance with her, and Avery was vehemently refusing to do so. "You are completely hung up on that girl…like I've never seen you hung up before."

"Yeah." I didn't bother denying it. "It would seem so."

"So what's up with that? You spend all this time with her, but you don't make a move."

I sighed. "It's complicated. She just got dumped hardcore."

"She doesn't seem all that broken up over it."

It was true. Aves had seemed a lot happier lately, but I'd seen her right when it happened. She was getting better, but her pain ran deep.

"It was my little brother who hurt her. How can I move

in on that?"

Owen shrugged and went back to the game. "Eleven in the corner. You said they were never together."

"Not technically, but they were like...I don't know how to describe it."

"Yeah, but there was nothing going on. For *seventeen years*? You weren't with her five minutes before you couldn't stop picturing her naked. That's how it's supposed to be. Fourteen in the corner."

Owen missed his shot, and as I lined up my next he said, "Sometimes it just works. It obviously does for you guys. She may think she's in love with your brother, but I've seen her look at you too. Trust me, the spark is there."

I missed my shot, definitely not on my game tonight. This conversation wasn't helping any. Then again, I was pretty sure that was part of Owen's strategy.

"Even if it is," I argued. "It won't happen until she lets go of the idea of my brother. That's what I'm trying to get her to do."

Owen sunk the last stripe on the table. "So try harder. You're Grayson Kennedy. You're the guy who upon turning eighteen got a personal invite to the Playboy mansion after spending less than twenty minutes in your first club."

I laughed. Some stories about me were exaggerated. That one wasn't.

"She's still trying to think of you as Aiden's older brother. Lay some serious mojo on the girl, and make her see you for you. Guarantee you she'll be like, 'Aiden who?' Eight ball, side pocket."

Owen went to line up his shot, and suddenly Avery was there. "Wait! Stop!"

Owen leaned up, startled.

Avery blushed but then forced herself to go stand next to Owen.

I watched, curious, as she assessed the table and then pointed to the corner pocket furthest from Owen—a different one than he'd called. "That one," she said. "The angle's wrong over here. Aim directly at the three ball. Give it a little bit of force, and it will bounce right off and straight into that pocket. It's a much clearer shot that way, I promise."

Owen raised a brow and Avery backed right off, turning a deep shade of red. "I mean, if you want to," she said quietly. "Sorry. I didn't mean to interrupt."

"You're sure?" Owen asked her.

She looked mortified that she'd said anything, but she nodded.

Owen looked back at the table and shrugged. "Why not?"

He lined up his shot, and it did exactly as Avery said it would. He sunk the eight ball with ease, and everyone around who'd witnessed the scene cheered.

"Aves!" I said, pouting a little. "Whose date are you anyway? You just won him the game!"

"Sorry." Avery looked at her shoes.

I laughed and pulled her to me. "It's okay. He was going to win anyway. He's by far the superior player."

"Hey, how'd you know about that?" Owen asked, still smiling from his victory.

Avery's face paled, and she stared at the floor again. "Um, I just…" She cringed. "It's all physics." The irony was not lost on me. "Angles, trajectory, mass, momentum, velocity…Newton's laws are—"

"Whoa, whoa, whoa, okay." Owen laughed. "That's enough geekspeak. I get it. But can you actually play the game, or do you just coach?"

Avery shrugged. "I'm all right."

I saw the gleam in Owen's eyes and wondered just how good Avery really was. The girl was the most modest person I'd ever met. I was sure she was downplaying her skills. I also knew there was no one more competitive than Owen.

"You up for a game?" he asked, exactly as I knew he would. "Say we make it interesting with a little friendly wager?"

Avery looked at the table and bit her bottom lip, contemplating. She wanted to give it a try. She looked back up at Owen and warily asked, "What are your terms?"

That's where I stepped in. "Oh, no, hold up! I get to pick the stakes."

"What?" Owen argued. "Why? I'm the one playing. It was my bet."

"Because," I said, "she won the last game for you."

Owen scoffed.

"She's *my* date," I continued. "*And* she gave me free reign over her social life, so I'm in charge of this bet."

Owen crossed his arms over his chest. "Fine. Name it."

I thought for a minute. We were gathering a small crowd now, so it had to be good. "Okay. Avery wins and you have to get from this pool table to your car without any clothes."

Avery gasped and tried to protest on Owen's behalf, but Owen doesn't know how to back down from a challenge. "Done. And if I win?"

I looked at Avery. It couldn't be anything too crazy—she was way too fragile, and I didn't actually know how good she was. I glanced around, looking for inspiration, and noticed the people in the corner. "If you win, Avery has to learn how to dance tonight."

Owen was going to argue that the terms weren't equal until Avery gasped again. The look of terror on her face said it all. Dancing may not have been a big deal to Owen, but for Avery it was going to be every bit as awful as streaking through a crowded party.

"Deal," Owen said and racked the balls. "I'll even let your little ringer break."

"Dancing?" Avery hissed in panic as I pushed her up to the table and handed her a cue. "Are you serious? I *can't* dance! Especially not in front of all these people! I will die!"

"Dancing does not kill people." I laughed. "If you're really that worried about it, then just beat Owen. Come on, Aves, you have to admit it would be highly entertaining to see him lose."

She was lined up in front of the balls now. When she looked at the table, she seemed to come back to herself. Pool was apparently a game Avery knew well and felt confident about. I was surprised by this and briefly wondered if Aiden knew this side of her. The possibility made me startlingly jealous.

"Okay," she whispered and lined up her first shot. "I agree to the terms."

And then I stood there and watched Little Avery Shaw run the table like a professional pool shark. She sunk ball after ball, analyzing every shot and never losing concentration. I'd never seen anything so hot in my life.

By the time she sunk the last ball, leaving only the eight left to sink for her win, even Owen was cheering her on. She stepped around the side of the table next to where I was standing. I bent down and kissed her cheek. "For luck."

She blushed and gave me a shy smile, then leaned over to line up her cue. It looked like a clear, easy shot. Just as she called it and pulled back her cue, I maybe, sort of, accidently-on-purpose let my hand slide down her back and over the curve of her butt. At my gentle squeeze, Avery let out a shriek and botched the shot so bad the cue ball jumped the table.

The entire room gasped, and then there was a mixture of laughs and angry shouts.

Avery stood there, face brighter red than I'd ever seen it, gaping at me in utter disbelief. "I just lost," she finally said. "You just made me lose."

"I know," I admitted, trying to look more repentant than I felt.

"By grabbing my butt!"

She was pissed. But was she mad that I'd copped a feel, or mad that I'd made her lose? I was hoping it was the latter.

"Yeah, I know, and I'm sorry. But seriously, Aves, you

working that table had to be the sexiest thing I've ever seen, and I simply couldn't let you win because I really, really, really want the chance to dance with you now."

Owen clasped a hand on my shoulder and laughed. "Well, I'm not going to argue. My dignity thanks you." He turned to Avery and put a hand on her shoulder too. "Try to go easy on the guy. It really was very sexy. I've never seen anyone play like that. You were amazing."

Aves blushed again and muttered, "It's a science club thing."

"Well, I'll be damned." Owen laughed again and squeezed Avery in a quick hug. "Now throw this pathetic loser a bone and go dance with him."

guilt

Avery

Dance. Grayson expected me to dance. And this wasn't middle-school dancing where you put your arms on your partner's shoulders and turn in a circle. This was fast, fluid, and sexy. I was doomed.

Though it could have been worse. At first, Grayson tried to pull me into the crowd, but Pamela and Chloe came to my rescue.

"No way! I won this dance fair and square. You guys go find your own partners!"

Pamela crossed her arms and gave Grayson a stern look.

"You cheated! As your punishment, Avery will be fulfilling the terms of her bet with Chloe and me. You said she had to dance. You didn't say who got to teach her."

"Yeah, she's ours now." Chloe tucked me behind her and pointed to the empty sofa. "You can go park it over there, Mr. Grabby McGrabbhands, and think about what you've done."

Grayson eyed the couch and then frowned. "You guys are putting me in time out?"

"Yes!" Pamela very much liked that idea. "You, Grayson Kennedy, have earned a time out. Now go on. Shoo."

Grayson looked worried for me, so Pamela eased up on him. "Avery is in excellent hands. Go find a drink or something and give us fifteen minutes to ease her into it."

Grayson wasn't happy, but eventually he looked at me and sighed. "You're right. It'll probably be easier for her to relax if it's just you girls." He smiled at me. "Remember it's supposed to be fun." He pointed to the couch that Chloe had just banished him to. "I'll be right over there doing exactly as I've been told and thinking very hard about what I did." He grinned then, so wickedly that I feared his next statement. "Remembering every glorious detail."

I know he got smacked on the arm, but I wasn't sure who'd done it, because I had to look away from him. The next thing I knew, I was being escorted into the middle of a crowd of people. Pamela whirled around to face me and grabbed onto my hands. "First, I just want you to relax. This isn't as hard as you think."

"Yeah," Chloe chimed in. "You'll be fine. It's a lot easier

to dance by yourself than with a guy."

I looked at them with gratitude and a sense of awe. I'd always assumed that the most popular girls in school would be the catty mean girls you read about. Those girls definitely existed, Pam and Chloe had even warned me of the worst ones, but so far I'd discovered that Grayson didn't put up with jerks, so the people at the top of the food chain with him were all really nice.

"You guys didn't have to do that," I said, even though I was more than grateful for their rescue.

"Oh, yes we did!" Chloe laughed. "Grayson gets away with murder. You were amazing out there. I can't believe he made you mess up like that. We girls have to stick together. Plus, I was really looking forward to Owen's strip show."

"More than that," Pamela said, "you are not ready to dance with Grayson."

Chloe moaned in agreement and fanned herself. "So true. He means well, but…" She shivered at a memory. "That boy is trouble without even trying."

I had no doubt about that. I looked at the couples dancing around us. That was enough to make me blush, and I was sure it would be worse dancing with Grayson.

"The best kind of trouble," Pamela said wistfully.

I was pretty sure I understood what that look meant. Not that it was surprising that she'd dated Grayson.

Pamela may as well have been named after Pamela Anderson, because she was destined to be a supermodel. She was five ten and a perfect hourglass. She had rich chestnut hair that flowed all the way to her waist and always behaved no matter what the weather was like. She was the ideal counterpart to a guy like Grayson.

"You guys dated, didn't you?" I asked.

She and Chloe both gave me guilty smiles.

"She was first," Pamela said of Chloe.

"But she lasted longer," Chloe said.

That surprised me. I was serious when I said I didn't think anyone had ever lasted longer than the weekend with Grayson. "How long did you guys go out?"

Pamela smiled. "Not as long as you."

"Me?" I gasped.

"It's been almost three weeks since New Year's Eve. I think that's some kind of record for Grayson."

"But Grayson and I aren't dating!"

"Please." Chloe laughed. "You are the closest thing to an actual girlfriend Grayson has ever had. You may not be kissing, but he doesn't even look at other girls anymore."

My jaw fell open and Pamela turned me around to face the couch. Grayson was sitting there watching us. He smiled at me and then yelled across the room at Pamela. "I don't see any dancing going on! Do I need to come over there?"

Pamela rolled her eyes at him and then turned me back around.

"You see?" Chloe teased. "He only has eyes for you."

"Completely smitten," Pamela agreed.

I felt a flutter in my stomach and told myself it was nerves. No way could it be actual butterflies. I was in love with Aiden, not Grayson. The two brothers couldn't be more different. Grayson and I had nothing in common. He just felt sorry for me. I was just one of the few girls he hadn't conquered yet. It had him curious, but his interest, if it was really there, would fade. I was just a shiny new toy at the moment.

"I think it's sweet," Chloe said, while Pamela shook her head and laughed.

"I think it serves him right. As many girls as he's made fall for him? It's about time he gets a dose of his own medicine."

I stumbled at the insinuation. "You think he's *fallen* for me?"

"Enough chatting," Pamela said with a knowing smile. "We're supposed to be dancing. So, first I want you to just hear to the music. Listen for the beat. Close your eyes if it helps."

She'd changed the subject, and that was fine by me. I couldn't think about Grayson anymore, so I closed my eyes. The song was one I didn't recognize, but the underlying beat was easy to pick out. The base was so deep that it vibrated in my chest. "Okay, so what am I supposed to do now?"

"Now? You just start to move."

Like that was any kind of instruction?

"Try bobbing your head in time with the beat," Chloe suggested.

"Or shifting your weight," Pamela said. "Bounce on your toes. You have to get your whole body moving."

I tried to copy their movements, but I felt like some kind of bobble-head whack-a-mole doll. There was no way what I was doing was considered dancing. My panic started rising, and I stopped moving. "Maybe some people just aren't meant to do this."

As I complained, someone stepped up behind me and I felt a pair of hands grip my upper arms. "You're overthinking it." Grayson's low, soft voice sent shivers up my spine. His hands slid up my arms to my neck, and then he buried his fingers deep in my hair, massaging my scalp. "You need to loosen up."

Slowly he pushed my head forward, rolling it from side to side until he brought it back to rest on his shoulder. He rubbed my shoulders next and then slid his hands down the entire length of my arms, leaving a trail of goose bumps where his fingers brushed along my skin.

I gasped at the sensations he was causing in me, and my eyes fluttered shut. He began to sway slowly, and my body, having melted into complete mush, matched his movements with more grace than I'd ever managed in my life.

"Dancing," he said, "is about feeling, not thinking."

Grayson lifted one of my arms above my head and rested it on the back of his neck. My fingers instinctively dug into his soft, thick hair. I hadn't told them to do that. I felt Grayson's cheek lift into a smile against the side of my head, as if he fully approved of my actions.

"Now we move together."

His arm came around my waist, and he suddenly knocked his knee forward into the backs of mine, forcing them to unlock. Unprepared for the shift in weight, I buckled, but he'd been ready for this. He caught me, held me up tight against him, and began moving us in an almost-circular motion.

My entire body heaved a shudder of pleasure, and then I drifted away from reality into a world where nothing existed except for the two of us.

Grayson moved artfully, seductively, to the music until I felt like we were one and the same with the beat. I had never experienced anything like it. I don't think I could have even imagined anything like it.

My body burned everywhere it was pressed against his, and every other part of me yearned jealously for the same feeling. I felt so relaxed I could almost sleep, and yet my heart pounded wildly in my chest.

"You're doing it, Aves," Grayson whispered against my ear. His breath caused more shivers to explode through me. "You're a natural."

"I'm not doing anything." I sounded dazed and a bit breathless. Probably because I was dazed and breathless. "You're doing this. I'm just letting you."

Grayson laughed low and dangerous. "The guy is supposed to lead, but he's only ever as good as his partner."

His lips touched my neck just behind my ear, and it felt so good I let out a barely-audible whimper. His entire body tensed in response. "Aves," he whispered in a strangled voice, "I want to kiss you."

My mouth responded before my brain had even processed his words. "I've never been kissed before."

Suddenly I was facing him, my hands resting lightly on his chest, his hands on my hips holding our bodies together in ways my mother would disapprove of. It was like the shower all over again except nowhere near as innocent. In fact, it wasn't innocent at all. I had to fight the urge to climb up him and wrap my legs around his waist.

Grayson stared down at me as if he were stranded in the Sahara and my lips were the last drops of water in his canteen. "I know," he said. "I want to be your first. Right here. Right now. Tell me it's okay."

His mouth was right there. His chest heaved as if his lungs were fighting for oxygen. His heart pounded beneath my hand. I could feel his need for me, but what surprised me was the intensity of my own desire. I wanted him to kiss me. With every fiber of my being I wanted his mouth on mine. I ached for it.

Even my heart begged for the connection, and that's when my dream world came crashing down. Suddenly I couldn't breathe. The room spun around me, and tears sprang into my eyes as I scrambled out of Grayson's embrace.

"Aves?" It took Grayson a minute to figure out what happened. "Crap! Aves, I'm sorry! You okay?"

"I need to get out of here!" I gasped. "I want to go home."

Grayson took me straight to his car, no questions asked, and headed back toward my house. He was quiet until the only evidence left of my freak out were the tears that continued to trickle down my cheeks.

"Aves, I am so sorry. I didn't mean to scare you. I didn't think. I just, I had you in my arms and you felt so good I—I didn't think. I don't think I've ever wanted to kiss someone so bad in all my life."

I turned my face to my window, leaned my forehead against the cold glass, and muttered, "I've never wanted someone to kiss me so bad in all my life."

The surprise of my confession caused Grayson to slam on the breaks. The car screeched to a stop.

"What? You *wanted* me to?"

I tried to wipe away the rest of my tears as Grayson pulled the car over to the side of the road.

"Of course I did!" I groaned. "Every single girl at that party tonight would have wanted you to kiss them had they been in my position. Grayson, I wanted you to kiss me so bad it physically hurt."

"Then…what happened? What was the problem?"

"The problem was that it was *you* I wanted! I wanted *you* to kiss me. Not Aiden."

Grayson opened his mouth to say something and then shut it again. He looked at me for a second as if I'd asked him some kind of trick question. "Um," he finally said. "You know, I'm really kind of okay with that. Relieved even."

"Well, I'm not! I feel awful!"

I started to cry again. I knew I sounded like I belonged strapped to a gurney in a room with padded walls, but I couldn't help it. I was drowning in a sea of guilt.

"I feel like I cheated on him. I know it's stupid. We weren't even ever together, but I loved him so much. I've dreamed about kissing him for so long. I have a million different scenarios written in my diary of how it would all play out when it finally happened."

Grayson chocked back a laugh. "You do not."

I gave him a grim look. I did. Detailed fantasies.

"I gave him my whole heart. It hasn't even been three weeks, and I barely cry about it anymore. I have all these new friends, and I do all these new things as if Aiden never even existed. As if he wasn't my whole universe for my entire life. It's like I completely moved on. And I didn't just almost kiss *anybody*. I almost kissed his *brother*. What kind of person does that?"

Grayson sat there with his hands on the wheel, staring out the windshield. Eventually he lifted his shoulders into a shrug. "Maybe you were never really in love with him." He turned to face me with a serious look. "What you felt tonight when we almost kissed, before you panicked, have you ever felt that with Aiden?"

I felt my cheeks heat up and looked at my lap. "I've never felt anything like that before. I didn't even know a person *could* feel like that."

"That just proves my point," Grayson said softly. "Aiden was your best friend. You loved him, but you weren't *in* love with him."

"Yes I was! I *am!*"

Grayson shook his head. "You're in love with the idea of him, but if you were really in love with him, you never would have gone on a date with me, much less let things go as far as they did."

We were quiet for a minute, and then Grayson tried a different approach. "Aves, you haven't done anything wrong. Aiden let you go. You should be able to move on. Even he would want that for you."

He was trying to make me feel better, but he was having the opposite effect. I started to cry again, so he reached over the center console and took my hand in his. He rubbed his thumb gently over the backs of my knuckles. The touch calmed me down some, which then of course made me feel guilty all over again and I started to cry harder.

"Please just take me home."

Grayson put the car back in motion. He didn't say another word as he drove me the last few miles to my house, but he held tight to my hand the entire way. Selfish as I am, I hung onto it, even though I'd basically just rejected him for his brother who had already made it clear he would never want me.

Even though the date ended a complete bust, Grayson, always the gentleman, walked me to my door.

"I'm sorry for losing it on you tonight."

Grayson tipped my chin up until he could see my eyes. I wasn't surprised by his understanding smile, but it hurt my heart. I didn't deserve his understanding.

"Let's consider it a good thing."

I frowned. How in the world was this mess I'd made a good thing?

As if reading my mind, Grayson grinned. "I think we've officially reached the fourth stage of grief. Perhaps tonight was more of a success than we thought, eh?"

I had to think back and repeat all the stages of grief, even though it should have been obvious. "Guilt!"

Grayson laughed. He stepped forward and dropped a feather light kiss on my cheek. "One step closer to acceptance, Aves."

He flashed me a beautiful smile and then winked at me as he climbed in his car and drove off.

science geeks

Grayson

Of all the stages of grief, so far guilt sucks the most. My date with Avery had been perfect. She looked amazing, she faced an insane party for me, and she was even having a good time! She severely dominated my best friend at a game of pool, making me the envy of every guy in the room...and then there was that dance.

She said she'd never felt anything like that, but what she doesn't know is that I hadn't either. Even with the countless girls I'd danced with, or done a whole lot more with, never in my whole life had I felt a connection like I did with Avery that night.

Forget my idiot brother. Avery was never meant to be with him. She was supposed to be with me. But, thanks to him, we didn't kiss that night. In fact the perfect evening ended so disastrous that I was worried she'd never speak to me again.

She didn't call Saturday or Sunday, and then at school the following week, she really distanced herself. She still sat with me at lunch and didn't pull away when I put my arm around her or held her hand, but it was different now. It was like she wouldn't allow herself to feel anything for me, not even friendship. I hated it.

She didn't come to school on Friday, and then I got another weekend of radio silence. I tried to call her a couple times, but I only got voicemail. When she didn't show up at lunch Monday, I really started to get worried.

"Maybe I should call her mom," I said for the umpteenth time. I looked across the table, hoping for some advice from Pamela and Chloe, but they were busy looking over my shoulder with wide incredulous eyes.

Owen and I looked at each other and then turned around at the same time.

Avery's friend Libby was standing there tapping a foot impatiently with her arms crossed. Her hair was in two buns on the top of her head that had tiny strands of hair sticking out from them in every direction. She was also wearing a giant hot pink t-shirt with a picture of a bored looking cat on it that said, "Do I look like I care about your problems?"

I'd seen this girl before at the science club meetings I

was forced to attend every Monday after school, but my friends had never been exposed to the holy little terror, and they clearly didn't know what to make of her.

When he could hold back no longer, Owen snorted and said, "Nice shirt."

Libby's eyes narrowed, and her hands went to her hips. "I make it work," she said matter-of-factly. She gave her head a little jerk and said, "Heard my girl Avery stomped you so hard in a game of pool last weekend that Grayson had to take pity on you before every college freshman at UVU saw just how small your junk is."

I burst out laughing. I couldn't help it. I laughed so hard I cried, and when I got a hold of myself, I realized that everyone at the table was laughing just as hard as I was. "Damn, Grayson!" Owen laughed and had to wipe tears from his eyes. "Where did you dig this chick up? Is she for real?"

"She's a nerd to be reckoned with, that's for sure," I said. "She's Avery's best friend. Libby, Owen. Owen, Libby. Never make the mistake of badmouthing cats in front of her. I think she used to be one in a past life."

We started to laugh again, but then Libby cleared her throat. She sounded more than a little agitated. "Are you coming after school today?"

I stopped laughing. A wave of panic surged through me. The science geeks had promised they'd never rat me out, but who knew how loyal they were? If Libby told these guys where I spent my Monday afternoons, I'd never live it down.

"I have no idea what you're talking about."

Libby rolled her eyes and said, "Are you going to *hang out with Avery* after school today?"

At the mention of Avery's name, I realized Libby must know what happened to her. "Why? Do you know where she is? What's going on with her? I tried to call her this weekend, but she wouldn't answer her phone. I was planning on going over to her house after school to check on her."

"Relax, lover boy, she's here. She's doing a make up math test right now since she missed school on Friday. She'll be around after school."

I was relieved, but at the same time I was a little hurt. "Do you know what happened? Why she won't answer my calls?"

Libby's face flushed with anger. "Your jerk brother is what happened! She was feeling all crazy guilty after last weekend, so she dragged me to his debate on Thursday."

Again, I was stung. She hadn't said a word to me about it. "Why didn't she ask me to come?"

"Something about not wanting to make Aiden feel bad. She doesn't want him to think she's replaced him with you."

Libby rolled her eyes again as if Avery's feelings were absurd. It actually helped to know that I had the little firecracker of a geek's approval.

"Anyway, we went to his debate because she felt bad that she hadn't talked to him in weeks. She was going on and on about how he'd said they were still friends and that she hadn't been supportive enough since he got a girlfriend. She was determined to be nice to Mindy and prove that she could be friends with them both." She snorted. "Please. As if anyone could be friends with that witch."

"So what happened?"

"What *happened?*" Libby laughed, but there was no humor in it. "We get there and the first break the team gets, Aiden comes over, and instead of saying hello, he asks what we're doing there."

I pulled in a long breath through my nose.

Libby nodded in agreement with my anger. "Avery almost cried right then and there," she said. "But instead she was all, 'You said this was important to you, so I just came to support you.' And then Aiden said, 'Aw, that's real sweet, Aves, but you shouldn't have come. I think it's upsetting Mindy, and you're kind of distracting the whole team.' The douche actually asked us to leave! Avery had a massive meltdown on the way home. She was so upset her mom called her out of school on Friday. They went to Vegas for the weekend just to get away."

"I'll kill him!"

"Please do," Libby said. "And put a foot up his ass for me while you're at it."

Next to me, Owen laughed again, but I couldn't appreciate Libby's colorful personality at the moment. I was way too pissed off. I was also worried about Avery. I couldn't imagine what that must have done to her.

"No wonder she didn't return my calls this weekend. I can't blame her if she never speaks to anyone in my family ever again."

I earned another eye roll from Libby, this one laced

with a don't-be-an-idiot undertone. "Oh, please! Avery's not answering your calls because she thinks having you around right now will make her feel worse, but that girl has never known what she needs."

"What *does* she need?"

Libby looked like she was going to smack me upside the head. "She needs *you*, moron! She needs you and all your glorious manly perfection to come and make her forget that that loser ever existed. She'll be in the science lab after school today, so come and get her and do *not* let her shut you out no matter what she says."

"Okay, but—"

"No buts! She needs you. You go. End of story. I will not let another Kennedy brother let her down."

By now I was trying to hide my smile, but I wasn't succeeding very well. "I got it boss," I said, giving Libby a mock salute. "Science lab. After school. Bring my glorious manly perfection."

Libby's posture finally relaxed a little. "Good."

"Definitely a cat in a past life," Owen muttered next to me. "But, like, a big scary one that ate people."

Libby eyed Owen critically for a moment with a raised eyebrow. "And I'm guessing you were probably Adonis…or a golden delicious apple because you are positively yummy."

Owen's jaw dropped to his lap while everyone else at the table fell apart from laughter.

Libby, in her all-business attitude said, "Call me if you need a date to the prom. Grayson can get my number from Avery." Then she spun on her heel and left the cafeteria.

Once she was gone Owen—with pink cheeks—turned back around and scowled. "That girl is a menace," he grumbled as he shoved his sandwich in his face.

It was true, but we all laughed at him again anyway. I even offered to lend him the keys to the condo in Park City for prom night. I almost got punched.

For the rest of the day all I could think about was getting to science club. I know, I know. I deserve to be shoved in a locker or given a swirly for that comment, but it was true. I needed to see Avery.

I was the first one there. Mr. Walden gave me a curious look when I bounded in the door and started pacing the length of the room, but he didn't ask.

After a minute Avery walked in with Libby and I froze. I'd never been afraid of a girl before, but I honestly had no clue what Avery was thinking, and I had no idea what to say to her.

I wasn't sure if I should approach her, but then I saw the what-are-you-waiting-for look on Libby's face, so I crossed the room, scooped her up into my arms and said, "I can't believe you and Kaitlin went to Vegas and didn't invite me. Not cool, Aves. I love Vegas!"

Avery let out this strangled laugh and finally threw her arms around my neck. When I set her down, there were tears in her eyes. I dried them for her and then dragged her over to a lab table and pulled out my project journal.

Avery cracked a small smile. "You're awfully excited for science today."

I shook my head. "Just anxious to get to the next stage

of the experiment. Please tell me we've finally reached anger. Libby told me what happened at lunch, and I am so ready for you to slap my brother around."

"Sorry." Avery sighed. "I'm definitely still in guilt."

"Well, I don't like the guilt stage. Seeing as how I'm the stupid source of your guilt, the result is very dissatisfying for me. There is way too much of you ignoring me going on. A whole weekend of absolute silence, Aves? Unacceptable. I've grown way too attached for you to ditch me for four days straight without so much as a text."

Avery sighed again. "I'm sorry. I didn't mean to worry you. I hope you at least had some fun on your weekend off from the Avery Shaw Experiment."

"No, as a matter of fact, I did not. But you know what does sound fun? Punching Aiden in the face. Or better, watching you punch Aiden in the face. So let's dump the guilt and bring on the anger. I've been waiting for this stage since the day he ditched you."

"Grayson, stop. I'm not going to punch him."

"I figure good old confrontation is the best way to trigger it. The debate team meets just across the building. We could all go together. We'll make it a science club field trip. We could have the geek squad film it for our final presentation at the fair."

"I resent your use of the term geek squad," Science Nerd Brandon said, throwing his bulky book bag down on the table across from Aves and me.

Science Nerd Levi plopped down next to him and said, "And I resent the fact that just because we're smart, you automatically assume we would know how to film your experiments. Not every geek is born with audio-visual knowledge."

Avery's science club friends all freaked me out and cracked me up at the same time. Seriously. I'm not sure how Avery and Aiden turned out seminormal when these are the kids they've been hanging out with for years.

"Brandon, your shirt is tucked into your pants. You *are* a geek," I pointed out. "It's cool, though. Everyone has their thing. I'm an athlete. You're a nerd. The world needs both to maintain balance. And Levi, there is absolutely no way you do not have extensive AV knowledge, am I right?"

Levi frowned but then sighed. "You are correct. I do know my way around video equipment, Mr. Dimwitted-jock-who-gets-tons-of-hot-girls-but-is-failing-high-school-science."

I laughed. "*Touché* on the stereotyping."

"Actually, I have my camera in my bag because Brandon and I are going to film the mixing of our next chemical compound for our experiment. I would be happy to capture on video the punching in the face of Aiden Kennedy if for nothing else than to show my posterity."

"Levi!" Avery gasped. "How can you say that? Aiden is your friend."

Brandon responded before Levi could. "He didn't just abandon you, Avery." He pushed his glasses up the bridge of his nose as if it made him look tougher somehow. "He quit on us all. I personally would love to see him get punched."

See? Science geeks aren't all bad. I gave my nod of

approval and then grinned at Libby. "Well, I know my girl Lib is in."

I held out a fist in Libby's direction. She frowned down at it. "My intelligence is evolved far beyond fist bumps. However, as the action would involve getting to touch your godliness for however brief a moment, I will allow it."

I had no idea how to respond to this, so I just said "sweet" and knocked my knuckles against hers.

When I looked back, Avery was watching us with a smile.

"Well, that just leaves Tara," I said, turning to the last geek of the group.

Tara was a freshman and somehow impossibly shier than Avery. She didn't seem to panic the way Avery does, but I guess a good-looking, popular senior such as myself was too much for her to handle.

Sweet girl, as far as I can tell, but she's never managed to say more than three words to me. The first time I spoke to her directly, she turned scary-red and almost fainted. She's gotten a little better over the last two weeks, but not much.

"You down to crash a debate club meeting and witness a little science in action?"

Tara couldn't get any words out this time, but she managed to nod her head, so I turned back to Avery. "The nerd herd has spoken, Aves. We're all here for you. Time to find your inner Rocky."

"You guys, no one is going to punch Aiden in the face, okay?" Avery rubbed at her temples like her head was starting to pound. "I'm not mad at Aiden. Hurt, yes; confused, very; but I'm not angry. Just because he hurt me, doesn't make it okay for me to hurt him back. He had every right to want a little space from me. I can also understand the need to pull away for his girlfriend's sake. If I was in her position and my new boyfriend had some girl that he'd been best friends with since birth, I'd be more than intimidated by her."

"Come on, Avery!" Libby groaned. "You are not actually condoning the way he treated you Thursday night, are you?"

"Lib. They wanted to win. If I really was causing contention and distracting their team, then I can understand them wanting me to leave. He was really polite about it, at least. I don't think he was angry that I showed up. I just feel bad that I messed them up. I heard they lost the debate."

"They lost the debate because they suck!" Libby said. "And Aiden sucks for having no regard for your feelings whatsoever! He's a jerk, Avery! How can you not be mad at him?"

"I'm just not, okay? Can we please drop it? I'm done working on the experiment for the day. We're supposed to be helping Grayson with his physics too, and he's got a make up quiz tomorrow on Newton's Laws."

This seemed to stop everyone. I wasn't sure why they were suddenly all staring at me until Brandon said, "Did you really fail a quiz on *Newton's Laws?*"

Okay. So they were staring at me because they all thought I was a moron. "What?" I asked a little defensively. "Like it's easy? 'Don't steal' I get. 'Red means stop' makes perfect sense. That Newton guy was smoking some serious crack when he made up his laws. When the hell will I ever use that stuff anyway?"

Avery patted my hand, but the rest of the nerds gaped at me and then shot each other a bunch of looks full of hidden meanings.

"This is not good," Levi said gravely. "Our president is dating a simpleton. Imagine if the guys over at Payson High find this out?"

"We'd lose all our street cred," Brandon agreed. "It's going to be bad enough having to take him to the science fair."

"Geeks have *street cred?*" I asked, only slightly offended. "And what will be so bad about having me at the science fair?"

"You're a popular. A beautiful people. A jock. No offense, but that's very bad for our reputation. Why do you think we were so happy to keep your presence in our club secret?"

I laughed in astonishment. *Who knew?*

"*I* happen to appreciate your beauty," Libby announced. "As well as your willingness to sink to our level of nerdiness for Avery's sake, even if you won't own up to it to your friends. Your devotion makes up for your less-fortunate qualities, but I'm sorry, we simply cannot have a member of our science club not understand the basic laws of motion. This is a science club emergency." Libby looked around the group. "It's time Grayson gets his first lesson in applied physics."

I was scared when the geeks dragged me out to the parking lot, but as it turned out "applied physics" was just some nerdy version of bowling. Actually, as far as punishment for failing a class goes, I could have done a lot worse than having to attend science club.

Once we were at the bowling alley, I caught Avery watching me as I laced up my bowling shoes. She did that every now and then during science club as if she still expected to see Aiden's face instead of mine. It always made me a little sad when I noticed her missing my brother, so I did my best to put a smile on her face every time it happened.

"What? No pool hall?"

Her answering smile was small, but it was real.

Libby snorted. "Not if you want a chance at winning."

Brandon puffed out his white-dress-shirt-clad chest and threw an arm around Avery's shoulders. "Avery is a master pool player."

"So I noticed."

The knowing look I shot Avery made her blush. It hadn't been her pool skills I noticed that night so much as the way she looked every time she leaned over the table to take a shot. I'd most likely have the same problem bowling today. Too bad she wasn't still wearing that dress.

I changed the subject before I started drooling. "So which one of you is the genius nerd bowling prodigy?"

"Actually, none of us are very good bowlers," Levi said. "It's just one of the more simplified ways to explain Newton's Laws of Motion. Athletes tend to be kinesthetic learners, so hands-on demonstrations usually work much better than lectures."

Kinesthetic learner? Was I supposed to know what that was?

Levi sighed, reading the confusion on my face. "Kinesthetic learners are people who learn by physically carrying out an activity rather than just watching a demonstration or listening to a lecture. Judging by the way you cannot ever sit still for more than five minutes, I am going to assume that you are either a kinesthetic learner or you suffer from ADHD."

He seemed to want an answer to this. "Uh…I'm not ADHD."

"Good. Then this should work."

"What should work?" I was starting to get scared again. If it weren't for the amused look on Avery's face, I might have bolted from the building.

"Since you are most likely a kinesthetic learner, for this study session we will have you physically put Newton's laws into motion."

"Uh…okay…" Sometimes their geekspeak was too much. Why couldn't he just say, "I think you're a moron, so I'm going to dumb it up for you with something I think you can relate to, like this dense inanimate object."

I wanted to be pissed off, but Avery was still sitting across the lane from me with this adorable grin on her face, so I couldn't find it in me to be offended by her smart friends.

"So, beefcakes," Libby said, startling me from my Avery staring. "How's about you pick up your ball, and let's get this party started. I happen to be a visual learner, so I am quite excited to have some eye candy to enhance my learning experience for a change."

That finally did it. I smiled. "You frighten me, Libby. You really do."

"She frightens us all," Brandon said, and then looked at me. "So, Grayson, my physics-ly challenged friend." He snorted. "Newton's first law of motion. What is it?"

I sighed, recognizing the beginnings of actual studying. I had hoped "applied physics" was really just code for "bowling," but I guess not.

Everyone was waiting for me to answer, so I tried to remember what I knew of Newton's Laws. "What goes up, must come down?"

When the entire group groaned, Avery took pity on me. "That's a rough translation of the law of gravity."

"Well, can we start with that one? Because that's the one I sort of understand. Gravity I get."

I got another round of groans for this, and Avery giggled as she explained why that was wrong.

"Gravity isn't one of the three laws of motion, but those are just as simple. Here…" At my look of doubt, she got up and handed me my bowling ball. "Is this ball going to throw itself down the lane?"

Was she messing with me? "Is this a trick question?"

Behind me, Tara giggled. I couldn't blame her. Even I knew I looked like an idiot now.

Avery gave me a sympathetic smile. "No. It's not a trick question."

"Um, okay. Then…no? It won't roll itself down the lane?"

"Exactly." She stepped aside. "So throw the ball."

I gave her another confused look but decided to trust her and chucked the ball toward the pins.

"Is the ball going to stop?" she asked.

"Not until it hits the back wall."

"Right."

At that moment the ball went crashing into the pins, knocking down all but two of them. It did in fact stop when it slammed into the back of the lane.

"There you go," Avery said as if that explained everything. "Newton's first law of motion. You understand it perfectly."

Everyone laughed at this except me. It was possible that I was more confused than I had been in class.

Avery picked up another bowling ball. "An object at rest…" she said and held up the ball,"will remain at rest unless acted on by an unbalanced force. Such as you throwing it. An object in motion…" She threw the ball down the lane toward the remaining two pins. "Continues in motion with the same speed and in the same direction unless acted on by an unbalanced force, such as hitting the back wall or the pins, or the friction of it rolling down the lane. If there were nothing to stop the ball, it wouldn't stop."

"You mean like how asteroids in space will just go forever until they crash into something?"

"Exactly!" Tara squeaked.

"So in other words, an object won't move unless

something gives it a push, and it won't stop unless something makes it."

The whole group of nerds clapped because I got it, but I felt myself frown. "What, you mean that's it? That's the whole law?" It couldn't be that simple.

"Yes. That's all there is to it." Avery laughed. Actually, everyone laughed.

"Well, why didn't Mr. Walden just say that in the first place?"

They all laughed again. So glad I could entertain them all.

Avery tried to stop laughing for my sake but couldn't quite manage it. She was so cute that it was worth looking like an idiot. "Come on, Einstein," she teased. "Pick up your ball. Laws two and three are just as easy. Once you have them down, we'll see if you're any better at bowling than you are at pool, and while we're at it, we can explain a few things like mass, momentum, velocity, force, inertia…"

I felt myself cringe. I kind of thought I'd find the smart-girl talk hot, but mostly it just freaked me out when she used words like velocity and inertia.

"Well, the bowling part sounds fun anyway." I grinned. "You up for a little friendly wager?"

Man, I loved watching her blush.

"No!" she said. "Definitely not. I've had my fill of friendly wagers, and *certain people* cannot be trusted to be gracious losers."

I laughed. The girl had a point.

failed experiment

Avery

After bowling I offered to help Grayson write a paper on his applied physics lesson at the bowling alley. "As part of science club if you write up a report on what you learned during our activities, you get to exchange it for a missed homework assignment or a failed quiz in Mr. Walden's class."

"Seriously? Mr. Walden doesn't seem that cool."

I sighed. "Grayson, most teachers are pretty cool when it comes to that stuff. Believe it or not, they actually want to see their students succeed. If they see you really applying yourself, they're usually pretty flexible."

"If you say so. But if we're going to write a paper, let's go to my house. My mom's been extra moody since she and Kaitlin got in their fight. Maybe if she sees you, it'll soften her up."

Grayson saw the expression on my face and said, "Don't worry, Aiden and The Leash Holder spend most of their time at her house."

I had no more excuses, so I called my mom and went to Grayson's house for the first time since winter break.

The Kennedy house, even though it's three times the size of the cozy two-bedroom my mom and I rent, has always felt like a second home to me. I even sort of had my own room. Well, technically it was a guest room, but I kept a bunch of my stuff there since I was over so much. It felt nice to be back, but at the same time it felt different.

"Avery! Hi, honey!"

Cheryl was sitting at her desk with a stack of papers piled practically to the ceiling. She was a private tax accountant, so January through April she basically lived in her office. The rest of the year she had a lot more freedom to hang out and do stay-at-home mom things like cook and hover.

I stepped into the office and gave Grayson's mom a hug. "Hi, Cheryl. I hope you don't mind that I came over. I know it's been awkward since New Year's."

"You're always welcome here, you know that. You're practically family. You're supposed to get in fights with my boys."

"I don't think it's a fight," I said sadly.

Cheryl's eyes softened. "You guys will work it out." She cast her eyes to Grayson and found her smile again. "But you and Grayson have sure become a lot closer, so all isn't lost, right?"

"Right." I wanted to feel happy, but I had to get something off my chest. "Cheryl, I am so sorry for what happened with Aiden. I just want you to know that I don't blame him."

Grayson snorted in disgust. I ignored him and continued the speech I'd been rehearsing since Grayson asked me to come over. "Please don't be mad at my mom anymore. I know she kind of went over the deep end with the protective bit, but that was my fault. I shouldn't have freaked out so much. I should have understood Aiden better. He didn't really do anything wrong and—"

"Avery, stop!" Grayson snapped, startling both Mrs. Kennedy and me. "You may not feel angry yet, but I do. I can't listen to you stand there and defend him. Aiden doesn't deserve it. He treated you like crap!"

"Grayson, calm down."

"It's true, Mom! He bailed on her for the science fair, and even though he said he still wanted to be her friend, he hasn't spoken to her in weeks. The first day back from school she sat down at their lunch table with all of their friends, and he was going to ask her to not sit with him anymore. He was going to make her leave her own lunch table!"

Cheryl gasped, and I quickly shook my head. "He was probably just going to ask me to switch seats with Libby so that I wasn't sitting right next to him."

"Like that's any better!" Grayson crossed his arms tightly over his chest and glared at me when I started to defend Aiden again. "Tell her what he did on Thursday."

"He had every right to—"

"No he didn't, Avery!"

"Grayson! Stop yelling at her."

"Mom! She went to watch his debate on Thursday to be nice and prove that she was okay with his choices. She wanted to introduce herself to Mindy and let them both know that she could be their friends. Aiden got pissed off that she showed up and made her leave. He acted like her wanting to be there for him made her some kind of psycho stalker!"

I didn't realize that my eyes were closed or that tears were leaking out of them until Grayson's arms came around me and he said, "No more tears, Aves. He's not worth it."

"Aiden really did all that?" Cheryl asked in a small voice.

I couldn't answer her, but I felt Grayson nod.

"Aiden is being a world-class jerk, and Kaitlin has every right to be pissed off at him. All of his friends are pissed off at him. I can't even stand to be around him because I just want to beat him senseless. You need to get over your fight with Kaitlin, and you need to have words with your freaking son. That bitch he's dating is turning him into an asshole."

"Grayson, watch your mouth!"

"Well, she is," Grayson muttered.

"Grayson." Cheryl sounded tired now. "I know your brother's girlfriend is…difficult, but would you please refrain from using those kinds of words?"

"Difficult?" Grayson scoffed.

"Yes. She's…she's…" Cheryl sighed and then threw her arms around me. "Oh, Avery, why couldn't it have been you? Grayson's right, Aiden's new girlfriend is…" She clearly wanted to use the B-word, but she couldn't let herself do it. "We all miss you so much."

She hugged me for a minute and then flopped back down in her desk chair. "I'm sorry. I've been so swamped that I haven't been paying enough attention. I'll talk to Aiden later, and Kaitlin. I promise."

"Thanks," I whispered. "But make sure Mom says she's sorry to you too. She was out of line with some of the stuff she said."

Cheryl's eyes sparkled with humor. "Oh, don't worry. I'll get an apology out of her. In the meantime, it's good to have you back." She glanced up at Grayson and smiled even bigger. "It's odd to see you with Grayson, but it's good to have you here."

Grayson tucked me into his side. "Better get used to it. I've taken a liking to the shrimp. She'll be back to her old visiting hours in no time."

Cheryl's smile melted into pure affection. She'd never admit it, but I've always thought Grayson was her favorite of the two. "What are you guys up to anyway?"

"I'm going to help Grayson write a paper. Science club took him bowling today and gave him his first lesson in applied physics. If he writes a report about it, he'll get extra credit."

All of Cheryl's affection was suddenly directed at me. "You are too good to my boys, Avery. Grayson told me what you did for him, talking Mr. Walden into letting him do the science fair instead of getting taken off the basketball team. That was pretty amazing of you."

I felt my cheeks get hot. "It wasn't that amazing. Grayson is still working hard for it, and he's helped me just as much. I really wouldn't have been able to do the science fair by myself."

"Still. Between my two boys, this family owes you."

I felt Grayson perk up beside me. "Actually, Mom, if you really want to do something nice for Avery, I had an idea about her birthday next weekend."

"My birthday?"

I was a little shocked. I hadn't said a word about my birthday to anyone. I was sort of hoping people would forget it this year since that's what I wanted to do. I didn't know how to celebrate my birthday without Aiden, and I wasn't particularly looking forward to learning.

Grayson squeezed my shoulders. "Aves, I know you're dreading it because Aiden said he didn't want to celebrate with you, but I'm not going to let you spend it home alone watching Shark Week reruns."

My face must have looked annoyed, because Cheryl laughed. The truth was, that was pretty much exactly how I'd been preparing to spend my birthday.

"Mom, would it be cool if we planned an overnight at the condo with just a few friends? Ski on Saturday and stay up all night watching movies? We'd be home Sunday evening. Wouldn't miss any school. Promise not to make a mess."

I didn't have to look at Grayson's face to know that his I'm-so-irresistible-you-can't-say-no-to-me smile was plastered there. Cheryl looked at the stacks of paper on her desk and sighed. "Hon, I don't have time to go up there for the weekend right now."

"Kaitlin could come."

I couldn't help but be touched by Grayson's persistence. "You'd really do all that for me?"

"Aves, this is your first birthday that will be celebrated the way a birthday should be—all about you. As your first real birthday, it's got to be epic, but I didn't think you'd like a big crazy party with a ton of people, so how about just a really fun overnighter with your closest friends?"

"Actually…" I started to cry then because that sounded so perfect. I'd been so bummed about my birthday. I'd just accepted that it would suck for the rest of my life. Grayson couldn't have known how badly I needed this. I needed my birthday to be awesome in order to prove that life really would go on without Aiden.

"I'm sorry. I've just been so emotional lately." I took a deep breath and wiped away the tears. "That sounds really nice, Grayson. I don't have to go up to the condo, though. We could just do something here and that would be good enough for me."

"Nonsense!" Cheryl said. She was looking at me with pity now, but I couldn't blame her. I was pretty pitiful right then. "If your mom can go up with you, then you're welcome to use the condo next weekend."

The way Grayson jolted next to me, I think he assumed she'd never go for it. "Awesome! You're the best mom ever!"

"Yes, thank you, Cheryl. I promise we'll be responsible."

Grayson jumped forward to give his mom a hug. When he pulled back, she nailed him with a suspicious gaze. "How many close friends are we talking about?"

"Just us, Owen, Pam, Chloe, and the nerd herd."

"The nerd herd?" Cheryl repeated while I gasped.

"You'd invite the science club? With Owen, Pam, and Chloe there?"

Cheryl finally understood and stared at her son in surprise. "My oldest son mixing social classes?"

"Oh yeah, Mom!" Grayson chirped. "It'll be an interesting experiment. Didn't you know? I'm all about social science now."

Cheryl laughed, but I could still hardly believe it. "You'd really invite Brandon, Levi, Libby, and Tara along with Owen, Pamela, and Chloe?"

All the playfulness left Grayson. The way he looked at me made my knees feel like shaking. Somehow I managed to keep them steady, though.

"Those are your friends, Aves. It's your birthday. I want you to spend it with all the people you care about, even if half of them are really weird."

I was too choked up to say anything.

"Well," Cheryl said. "I think it will be a good experience for all of them. Make sure Kaitlin can go. Boys and girls sleep in separate rooms and absolutely no alcohol. If

Kaitlin finds even one drop of it, you will all be murdered."

"Deal," Grayson said.

"Then you have my blessing. Now go away so that I can get some work done."

Grayson dragged us out of there so fast that I thought he was afraid Cheryl would come to her senses and take back the offer. He was so excited about my birthday that it took a while for him to settle down enough that he could focus on writing his paper. It ended up taking longer than we expected.

We were on Grayson's bed, and when I stretched and lay back on his pillow, he closed his notebook. "I can write the conclusion myself. We can be done now."

"No, it's okay," I said, but as I did, I yawned again.

"It's getting close to nine. I should get you home anyway."

"Okay."

I made no effort to sit up.

Grayson shoved his books on the floor and then lay down next to me. "We didn't get to work on our experiment at all today. I'm sorry we wasted the whole day on me."

"That was not a waste, and it's okay. We don't really have anything else to work on right now. We haven't done any kind of test for a while, and we're still stuck in guilt."

Grayson chuckled. "Should have let us take on the debate team today. The geek squad was ready. Would have been an awesome field test."

I sighed. "It goes against my nature to want to hurt him, Grayson. I have no idea how we're going to reach anger."

"Well, I don't understand how you aren't angry. He was totally wrong, and he hurt you so much. I think you're afraid of hurting him the way he hurt you, so you're suppressing your anger. I think it's there, and if you don't deal with it eventually, one day you'll just explode."

I had no idea what to say. He was probably right. He'd been right about everything so far. "So what do you suggest I do, oh wise, unbiased decision maker of the Avery Shaw Experiment?"

Grayson leaned up on his side, propping himself up on his elbow, and looked down at me with a serious expression. "Honestly?"

"Yes. Be honest. You're right about guilt being the worst stage so far. I hate feeling so bad all the time. If you have any ideas, I'll do whatever you think I need."

"Okay." Grayson's eyes locked on mine. "I think you should kiss me."

My heart stopped. "Um…"

You would think that after dancing together and almost kissing him then I would be able to control my blushing and anxiety, but as I lay there on his bed with him gazing intently down at me, my breathing became really shallow. I had to look away from him.

"How will that help?"

"I think you're too close to the project right now. You're so attached to the idea of these stages that you're like a self-fulfilling prophecy. You know you're in the guilt stage, so you keep feeling it. You're obsessing over it and making it worse. You also know anger is coming next, but you're scared of being angry, so subconsciously you're not allowing yourself to feel the anger."

"Okay. I suppose I can see that, but…" I had to forcibly slow my breathing down. "How will kissing you change that?"

I finally managed to look at Grayson, but it didn't matter because his eyes were trained on my lips. I bit the bottom one nervously, and the action made him swallow really hard in response.

He wet his lips and forced himself to answer my question. It clearly took him effort to pull his focus back to the conversation. "It's something unexpected. It'll take the steps out of order. You're not supposed to be at a kissing-some-one-new stage yet. You'll feel things your brain doesn't think you should be feeling. I'm hoping it might throw your mind off enough to sort of hit the reset button, you know? Maybe it will make your heart take point for a while instead of your head. Then you'll react to things more naturally and get back on track."

I tried to find a way to argue but couldn't come up with anything. Maybe I didn't want to. "Actually, your logic is pretty solid."

One corner of Grayson's mouth curved up. "I thought it sounded good."

We sat there for a heartbeat in silence. His eyes were still focused on my lips, and I could swear he was just a tiny bit closer than he had been before.

"But it would be my first kiss," I said. My voice wouldn't work above a whisper anymore.

"Even better. Twice as distracting."

"Shouldn't my first kiss be special, with someone I care for instead of as part of a scientific experiment?"

Grayson's eyes finally snapped back to mine. "Someone you care for? I'm hurt, Aves," he teased. "Are you saying you don't care for me?"

I rolled my eyes, grateful for the return of his playfulness. That was a lot easier to deal with than his intensity. "Of course I care about you. You know I do." I was able to smile and tease him back. "You're my unofficial gross older brother, remember?"

"You think *I'm* gross? You consider me a brother, but you still kissed me anyway. *That* is gross."

"What are you talking about? I didn't kiss you."

He came at me fast, but when his lips pressed down on mine, his movements slowed to a near stop, as if he were savoring every second of this moment.

For years I'd imagined what a kiss would feel like. It turns out my imagination is severely lacking. I figured it would feel soft and warm and maybe tingly, but I didn't really understand what soft, warm, and tingly actually felt like until Grayson Kennedy showed me.

The kiss was short, but so delicate and tender. Not at all the fire and passion and mess of tangled tongues you read about in books. In fact, there was no tongue. It was just two pairs of lips meeting for the first time.

It felt like he was being careful with me, and I really appreciated that. Instead of panicking, as I'd assumed would happen, his touch calmed me, and I was able to simply experience it. My mouth opened instinctively, and he immediately caught my bottom lip in his. He lingered only long enough to give me the chance to react with a small kiss of my own. When I finally did, he smiled against my lips and leaned back.

"Now you've kissed me," he said, his eyes alight with more than just mischief. "Still think I'm gross?"

"I…I…" I was flustered but also still somewhat up in the clouds—the peace and panic inside me were at war with one another. "I don't know what I'm feeling right now."

Grayson grinned. "I think that means it's working. Maybe we should do it again."

"Again?"

"We need to make sure we really test this theory as thoroughly as possible."

"We do?"

"Yes, Avery. I hereby demand as a completely impartial outside observer with absolutely no personal interest in the outcome of this experiment that you need to kiss me again. Right now. For purely scientific purposes, of course."

"For science?"

"Yes! In the name of science!"

He gave me a questioning look, and I blushed of course, but I surprised us both when I giggled. "I suppose I did give you permission to run this experiment however you deemed necessary."

Grayson grinned so big his rare dimple was out on full display. "Trust me, Aves, it's definitely necessary."

The second kiss was nothing like the first. I thought

that one had been amazing—it had been the perfect first kiss—but this second kiss was mind-blowing in an entirely different way. This one *was* heat and passion, and a certain sense of impatience that suggested he'd waited way too long for it.

Grayson rolled forward slightly so that our bodies were pressed together, and I felt that familiar explosion of heat that had overcome me when we'd danced. As he rested his hand on my cheek, my arms found their way around his neck.

After a moment Grayson pulled back and teasingly asked, "Gross?"

For the first time in my life I didn't feel shy. "Definitely," I said, pulling his face back down to mine. "Very, very gross."

Grayson laughed and then brushed my new bangs back and kissed me again. This time I was pretty sure he wasn't going to stop anytime soon. I was okay with that.

He'd just slipped his tongue into my mouth, and I'd just decided that french kissing rocks when Aiden's voice broke through the bubble we were in. As per house rules, we'd left Grayson's bedroom door open. We'd both forgotten about that, seeing as how neither of us ever suspected we might want the privacy, so there was no time to pull apart before Aiden walked in.

"Hey, Grayson, I just thought you'd be happy to know that I broke up with—" He broke off midsentence with a gasp.

I shot up to a sitting position. This time instead of the

blood rushing too my face, it drained from it.

Grayson sighed and pulled himself into a sitting position as well. "Aves, you were doing so well, don't freak out now." He looked at his brother, and in a dry voice said, "About time. Would you mind shutting the door on your way out?"

Aiden didn't leave. His face flushed an angry red. "How dare you take advantage of her! It's *Avery*, Grayson! Of all the girls in the world, how could you screw with *her?*"

I could hear the forced control in Grayson's reply. "I wasn't screwing with her."

"No," Aiden spat. "You were just trying to screw her."

I couldn't believe he'd just said that. "Aiden!"

At the sound of my voice, Aiden turned his fury on me. "How could you fall for it, Aves? As many times as you've seen him do this to other girls?"

I gasped. His disappointment and disgust cut me all the way to my bones.

"I thought you were smarter than that, but I guess you're just like every other girl after all. Congratulations. How does it feel to be Grayson Kennedy's latest conquest?"

There was no stopping the tidal wave of tears that flooded from my eyes. I scrambled off the bed and ran past them out the door. I hoped Grayson would bring my backpack to school for me tomorrow, because there was no way I was going to go back for it.

"Avery!" Grayson shouted. I didn't stop, but as I flew down the stairs I heard him shout, "Idiot! How many times do you have to break her heart?"

I burst into the office a sobbing mess and threw myself at Cheryl. "Avery?" she gasped, wrapping her arms around me.

"Can you please take me home?"

"Of course, honey. What happened?"

"I just want to leave."

Cheryl reached around me to grab her purse, but Grayson stopped her. "Let me, Mom," he said quietly.

Cheryl searched my face for signs of approval, but Grayson didn't give me a chance to protest. He pulled me from his mother's arms. "Aves, that's not what that was about. I swear you're not just another girl to me."

I wasn't so sure about that, but that wasn't what I was so upset about. "He hates me, Grayson! Did you see the look on his face? He was disgusted with me!"

"Don't let him ruin what just happened. It wasn't disgusting. It was amazing and special. Hell, it's been practically inevitable since New Year's Eve."

I shook my head furiously. "What it was, was a failed experiment. It didn't reset anything! Now I just feel guiltier than ever!"

I turned to Cheryl, who was watching us at a complete loss for words. She'd probably pieced together what had happened, but when I turned to her and asked her if she would take me home now, she didn't say anything about it. She simply grabbed her purse and ushered me past Grayson out to her car.

scientific method

Grayson

Damn Aiden to the very deepest depths of hell. Avery was back at square one with her heartbreak, and I was back at square one with her. We'd had this amazing moment—we'd shared her first kiss—but she couldn't even muster up a smile for me the next morning at school.

That whole week I couldn't get much more out of her than two- or three-word sentences. She was too busy watching Aiden from a distance. He'd rejoined the science squad for lunch, but it was clear he wasn't really part of the group anymore. I was sure Avery blamed herself for it.

I also know she wanted to talk to him, but every now and then he would look our way and glare with such hatred it would make Avery sick to her stomach, and she couldn't bring herself to speak to him.

His death looks were all for me. I know because he told me so. He accused me of stealing his best friend. I told him it wasn't stealing if he'd already thrown her to the curb like a piece of garbage. We almost came to blows over it. The only reason I didn't punch him was because it would hurt Avery, and she'd been hurt enough. But again, Avery saw his anger and blamed herself.

On Friday, Aiden left the cafeteria early. I hadn't been paying attention, so I wasn't sure what Avery meant when she said, "He didn't eat any of his lunch."

"What?" I asked.

I followed her worried gaze just in time to see my brother skulk out of the room.

"Aiden," Avery explained. "He didn't eat any of his lunch. He just threw it out. Has he been eating at home?"

"I don't know. He hasn't come out of his room at all this week except to pick fights with me. If he's having a hard time right now, I say let him suffer. Maybe it'll make him think twice before he acts like such a jackass in the future."

Avery set down the apple she'd been nibbling on. "He's all by himself right now, Grayson. *You're* mad at him. He doesn't want to have anything to do with *me*. Our friends tolerate him, but it's clear they've all taken my side; and now that he's broken up with Mindy, he doesn't have any of his new friends, either. I snuck into his debate yesterday for a few minutes just to check on him, and it looked like Mindy had turned his whole team against him. He doesn't have any friends anymore."

"He did it to himself, Aves."

"I know, but I still feel bad for him."

Avery sighed.

"Why don't we go do something fun tonight?" I suggested. "Or we could do something for the experiment. We haven't worked on it in forever."

Avery cut me a grave look. "Working on the experiment is what made this mess so bad in the first place."

It was hard for me not to lose my patience. I was so tired of this. I'd been mostly joking the night I asked her to kiss me for scientific reasons. Yeah, I really thought it would help her, but mostly I just wanted to kiss her. I thought she understood that, but she'd clung to the idea that our kiss was nothing more than a case of trial and error ever since it happened. I guess she thought if she told herself it meant nothing, then maybe Aiden wouldn't be so disgusted with her for kissing me...you know, since clearly he considered me the ultimate scum of the universe.

The problem was that our kiss hadn't meant nothing. Not to me. I'd wanted it so bad. I'd waited for the exact right moment when I was sure it was what she wanted too, and I'd thought of nothing else since it happened.

"Do you regret kissing me?" I blurted suddenly, surprising everyone present, myself included.

Avery's face paled as she took in all the curious stares. She looked down at her lap without answering me. I felt bad for the audience, but now that I'd started this I had to finish it. "I know you feel guilty about it because of Aiden, but do you regret it? Do you wish I hadn't done it? Do you think I played you?"

She flinched at the last question and looked up at me with her big blue eyes full of concern for me. "Of course I don't think you played me. I know that's not what that kiss was about. You were trying to help me. Just because it didn't work doesn't mean I'm mad at you for it."

"But do you regret it?"

It took her a minute to answer. She couldn't meet my eyes, and when she spoke, it was so quiet that if she hadn't shaken her head, I might not have understood her.

"No. I don't think so."

When I let out a breath, I realized how much I'd needed that answer. I didn't like the "think so" part, but at least it wasn't a yes.

"Good," I said. "Because I wouldn't take it back for anything."

She looked up at me again, surprised by my confession, and I asked her something I'd never asked any other girl before. "Will you be my girlfriend, Avery? Officially, I mean?"

Avery wasn't the only person around the table to gasp. I did my best to hold her eyes with mine so that she wouldn't pay attention to the people watching us and freak herself out.

"But…" Her shock turned to confusion. "You don't do the girlfriend thing. You always say that. You've never had one before."

"A guy can change his mind if the right girl comes along, can't he?"

"Um…"

"I know I have a reputation."

Someone snorted and a few others snickered, which really didn't help my case any, but I was determined. "I've never been interested in a girlfriend before, Aves, but you make me want to try it. Will you give us chance?"

Pam and Chloe both sighed like I'd just said the most romantic thing in the world, but Avery didn't melt like they did. She cast a quick glance toward the door that Aiden had just walked out of.

I suddenly wanted to punch something very, very badly. "You can't possibly still want him."

"It's not that," she said. "I'm just really mixed-up emotionally. I'm scared and confused and still just really, really hurt. I'm not over it. I'm not over him."

"How can you not—"

"I want to be," she said quickly, not letting me finish. "I try to be. I even thought I didn't want him anymore for a while, but then he broke up with his girlfriend and some sick part of me that loves torture got hopeful."

"Aves—"

She shook her head, still not letting me interrupt. "It'll never happen. I know that. I'm past denial, remember? I hate that I feel this way. I hate that he can still affect me."

She searched my face for understanding. "I would love nothing more than to say yes to you right now, but it would be in hopes that it would help get him out of my head, and that wouldn't be fair to you. You deserve so much better than that. You deserve a girl whose whole heart is in it, not some permanently-damaged mental case."

I had to read between the lines. She'd said no, but it wasn't really a rejection.

"Okay," I said. "Let's say, hypothetically, that you weren't damaged goods. If my brother weren't in the picture, if I had been born an only child, if all you knew was me, would you consider being my girlfriend then?"

I braced myself for a real rejection.

"Grayson," she said tiredly. "If that were the case, I wouldn't have to consider it. I'd probably already be naming our future babies."

I am not often taken by complete surprise, but that comment had me reeling.

Avery gave me a sad smile and slipped her arm around me. It was the first hug she'd given me since we kissed. "You have no idea how amazing you are. This is about me. I promise."

I hugged her back and felt my smile spread from ear to ear. "All you had to do was say you weren't ready," I teased, wanting to lighten the atmosphere before she started dwelling on how miserable she felt again. "I can wait. We'll get your heart all nice and patched up and *then* you can say yes to me."

"If you actually manage to fix my heart, I'll say yes to whatever you want."

Avery was so innocent I know she didn't mean that

statement the way my brain interpreted it—she probably didn't even realize it could be taken in such a way—but still, my mind went from zero to dirty in no time flat.

"*Anything* I want?" I laughed. "Will you do me a favor and put that in writing?"

She finally caught my meaning, and I was rewarded with that cute little embarrassed shriek of hers. "Grayson!" And the rosy cheeks. "You know I didn't mean *that!*"

"Believe me, I know," I said mournfully. "But you did mention having my babies, so I know you've at least thought about going there with me. I'd say there's hope for my future."

"Grayson! Oh my gosh! Stop!"

"Okay. Okay. Fine." I really didn't want to stop. I loved getting her all worked up. "I'll stop on one condition."

"What?" she asked so warily that I laughed at her.

"You can't let Aiden ruin your birthday weekend. Don't smart people know how to compartmentalize? File him away in your stress-about-later folder, and starting right now, just think about how much awesome fun we are all going to have tomorrow."

The mention of our skiing overnighter got Owen, Pam, and Chloe all talking before Avery could respond, but their excitement perked her up. "Make sure you all pack your swim suits," I said. "Our building has a sick indoor pool and a hot tub." Then, because I couldn't resist, I leaned down and whispered in Avery's ear. "Unless you'd rather just hit the shower together again. But then it's your turn to be naked."

Avery shrieked again, just like I hoped she would.

That conversation at lunch was the most life I'd seen in Avery since my brother caught us kissing. I wanted to make sure her mood stayed happy for her birthday the next day, so I showed up at her house after school prepared to keep her distracted the rest of the day.

"Grayson!" She was more excited to see me than I'd expected. "What are you doing here?"

I held up my science journal. "We only have a month until the science fair. We have work to do."

Avery smiled and opened the door wide to let me in. "I don't know why Mr. Walden was worried about you being my partner," she said as she directed me into her living room. "You've been more of a slave driver than a slacker."

I rolled my eyes. "A slave driver? We haven't worked on this since I took you to that party weeks ago."

Avery gave me a confused look. "Didn't you write up an entry in your journal about the kiss?"

"Why?" I eyed her journal as she took it from her bag and set it out on the coffee table in front of us. "Did you?"

I was hoping to fluster her, but instead she frowned again. "Of course I did. We have to record all of our experiments."

I resisted the urge to bang my head against a wall.

Avery paused and then sent me a panicked expression. "You *are* recording our experiments in your journal, aren't you? Because we need your viewpoints on everything to keep the integrity of this project."

"Aves, relax. Yes, I've kept my dumb journal up-to-date.

I blabbed all about our kiss in it, okay?"

Suddenly curious about what she'd written on the topic of our kiss, I snatched up her journal and flipped to the last entry. I thought she'd freak, but she just smiled at me and asked if I wanted something to drink.

I assumed that was permission enough, so I read her entry as she went in search of some soda. All I can say is no freaking wonder she considered our kiss an experiment. I flipped back through all of her entries and found every step of this project mapped out in detailed outlines.

"What is this?" I complained when she came back and handed me a Sprite. My voice conveyed all the confusion, disappointment, and horror I felt.

"My journal?" she asked, confused.

"This is not a journal. This is…it's a freaking textbook. Where's all the good stuff?"

"What do you mean?"

"You know, all the girly stuff." I kicked my voice into my best falsetto. "OMG I got my first kiss tonight! It was AH-MAZING! Grayson Kennedy is so hot!" Bringing my voice back to normal, I flipped the open book so she could see it. "There's not one single exclamation point, smiley face, or heart scribbled in this thing."

Avery burst into the biggest laugh I'd ever heard from her. She went into full hysterics.

"What?" I demanded.

"It's not a diary, Grayson!" She had to wipe tears from her eyes. "It's a scientific study!"

I failed to see the difference.

Avery looked at my face and fell into another fit of laughter. Once she could talk again, she opened the book—I refused to call it a journal—to the last entry and started pointing things out. "It's a log book of all the work we've done through the experiment."

"It looks like a bunch of outlines. What is this pattern you're using?"

Trying very hard to get her giggles under control, she pointed at the first heading. "It's called the scientific method," she said. "It's the process by which science is carried out. Basically it boils down to question, hypothesis, prediction, test, and analysis."

"What does that even mean?"

Aves got that look on her face that she'd had when she handed me a bowling ball and told me about Newton's Laws. It was a little pitying, completely amused, and slightly excited. I could tell she liked teaching. She'd be a great teacher, actually.

"Here." She sat down next to me and opened the book back to the kiss entry. "First you have to have a question. In this case, yours was, 'Why can't Avery move on from the guilt stage?' Your hypothesis was that I was self-fulfilling the feelings of guilt and subconsciously repressing the anger. Next you predicted that if I could be forced to feel something out of sequence, it might break the cycle and put me back on a more natural path. You tested it by kissing me. The analysis is the result of the test. In this case the experiment failed because afterward, despite momentarily experiencing feelings of acceptance and happiness, the second I was faced with the original problem, I went right back to guilt."

I had no idea what to think. I read her "analysis" again and frowned. "Geez, Aves, you sure know how to bleed all the romance out of a kiss. I must have really sucked performance-wise if *this* is how you remember it."

"Grayson, this journal is a record of our scientific research. It doesn't depict my *personal* feelings on the matter." Avery's face crept into fire-engine territory. "Of course you didn't suck. I think that might be impossible. I couldn't have asked for a more perfect first kiss."

She really looks so adorable when her face is all pink like that. She was so close to me too and smelled completely mouthwatering as always.

"I don't know. The fact that you could even look at that kiss analytically after it happened means it wasn't good enough. I think you'd better give me another chance to do it better."

I couldn't get my eyes to look anywhere but her lips—those lips that I just had to taste again. Right now.

I started to lower my face to hers, and she quickly leaned forward out of my reach. "Actually," she said, "I think I'd better take a look at *your* journal."

"Oh, no you don't!" I forgot all about kissing Avery and scrambled for my journal before she could get her analytical hands on it.

"But this is going to be turned in. It's going to be judged, Grayson, and now you have me worried now that there's not enough actual science being recorded in it."

"Are you kidding? There is so much science going on up in here that I deserve a freaking PhD."

"Then why can't I see it?"

There was no way I was showing her this journal filled with crap about how I was getting a crush on her, and how I love to make her blush, and how dancing with her had blown my mind beyond all reason. Especially not after seeing her stupid scientific method. No freaking way. I was going to have to rewrite the whole thing from the beginning before I turned it in.

I tucked the book more securely into my arms. "Because I am the outside, unbiased observer, remember? Reading my thoughts before it's over would completely taint the whole experiment."

Avery glanced at the journal again but stopped insisting. "You're right. I'm sorry. But will you let me read it after the science fair?"

You see? This is why journals are lame. How did I turn into such a girl?

"I guess that depends on the outcome of the experiment."

Avery actually pouted at me. It was freaking adorable. Every bit as cute as when she blushed. Maybe a little sexy even. "Fine," she said. "But you do realize that people are eventually going to read it, right? The judges and Mr. Walden? The book will be on display at our booth for anyone visiting the science fair."

I crossed my arms defiantly. "Well, then once it's on display, you can flip through it all you'd like. For now it's off limits. But it does need some more entries, so we need to get working on this anger business. I have a few *theories* that need to be *tested*. See? I'm all over this science business."

anger

Avery

Grayson wasn't joking when he said he had theories to test. He'd come prepared.

He said he still thought the best way for me to finally get mad was to lock Aiden and me in a room together and make us battle it out. When I said no to that one, he showed me his backup plan.

I'm not much of an angry person. I never have been. Easily stressed out to the point of hyperventilation, sure. But getting in fights? Never.

Grayson decided that if I could get really angry, for any

reason at all, that might work as a catalyst for the all the *pent-up rage*—his words, not mine—I was harboring for his brother. He'd looked up ways to make a person irritable on the Internet and then declared he planned to annoy the crap out of me until I *unleashed a shit-storm of fury* on him. Again, that phrase was all Grayson.

According to Google, the easiest way to make someone irritable is to overstimulate them. Grayson started by making me down a four-pack of Red Bull. Then he locked us in my bedroom with a strobe light, turned up some kind of angry death-metal music and pelted me with raisins. That didn't work, so he pulled a water gun out of his backpack.

When he refused to stop squirting me unless I made him, I finally lost my sanity and launched myself at him. I wrestled him for the gun, but that just turned into him tickle torturing me until I almost peed my pants.

Instead of angry, I ended up soaked with raisins stuck in my hair and pinned beneath Grayson on my bed. This proved to be too tempting for Grayson's next-to-nonexistent restraint. He kissed me, and even with the strobe light and the death metal blaring, I kissed him right back. We kept it up for quite a while, and that's how my mom found us when she got home from work.

Grayson tried to tell her it was in the name of science. I blamed all the Red Bull. Neither excuse was acceptable for my mom. She sat us down and forced us to tell her exactly what was going on. I showed her my science journal about our experiment, hoping it would make her take pity on me. I think it did, but she didn't really calm down until after she read Grayson's journal.

I don't know what Grayson had been writing in that thing, but whatever it was, it couldn't have been as scientific as he claimed it was. Mom read his "prologue," then ordered the two of us to go cook dinner, while she curled up in a chair and devoured the rest of the journal like it was one of her soap operas. I heard her laugh out loud many times, and when she finished, I noticed a small pile of tissues sitting on the end table.

Mom had always loved Grayson, but after reading his journal, I think she might have actually fallen *in* love with him. For me, I mean. She completely forgave us for making out on my bed with the door closed and pretty much acted like we were going to be married one day.

She did, however, manage to threaten him within an inch of his life if he so much as laid one finger on me during our overnight the next day. I think she planned on duct taping us both to our own beds.

The next day on the slopes, Mom and I ended up on a ski lift together, and I couldn't help asking, "What the heck is in Grayson's journal?"

Mom smiled at me with this love-struck twinkle in her eyes. "He's such a good boy, isn't he? I'm so glad he's been there for you."

I sighed. No way was she going to spill the beans. Grayson had her completely wrapped around his little finger.

After a minute of silence, mom sucked in a big gulp of the cold, fresh mountain air. "You know, Avery, I owe you an apology." Her voice was really small all of a sudden. "You and Aiden both."

"For what?"

I looked up, shocked to see that my mother was crying. "You guys always got along so well that Cheryl and I never once thought about what we were doing to you kids. What you and Aiden are going through right now is our fault."

"Mom." I tried to give my mom a big hug. My arms wouldn't go all the way around her thanks to our coats, but I still managed to get a good grip on her. "Don't blame yourself. Aiden and I will get through this somehow. You need to stop being mad at Cheryl. Tell her you're sorry. Aiden hurt me, but it wasn't her fault. And it's not yours."

"I'm not mad at Cheryl anymore," Mom admitted. She took her gloves off to swipe at her tears. "I'm as much to blame as she is. We didn't set the proper boundaries for you kids growing up. We had no idea what we were doing to you."

"You didn't do anything to us except give us a loving environment and a great example of a healthy friendship."

My mom smiled a sad smile at me. "Maybe, but your relationship with Aiden wasn't healthy, and neither of us noticed."

This news was shocking to me. "What do you mean?"

"Something Grayson said in his journal made me realize that maybe you needed this. I'm sorry you got hurt. Aiden didn't handle the situation very well at all, but I think he did the best he knew how, and I agree with him that the two of you needed some distance between you."

When I gasped, my mom's tears returned. "Avery, you've changed so much since winter break. You're really growing into yourself. You've gained confidence, and you don't have as much trouble with your anxiety." She ran her eyes over me and brushed her fingers through my new bangs. "Honey, you glow now in a way you never did before. You're growing up."

I felt myself blush and tears sprang up in my eyes. My voice was thick when I replied. "Thanks, Mom."

We were almost to the top of the mountain, so my mom wiped her eyes one last time and then put her gloves back on. "I love you so much, Avery. It hasn't been easy raising you on my own. I'm just one person, and I'm far from perfect."

"You're perfect for me," I said, hugging her again. "I don't need anyone else."

"Yes, you do. You need your friends. You need me the most, but you also need your friends. And..." She hesitated as if suddenly feeling awkward about something. Then she said, "You need Grayson."

I felt my face heat up so much I figured I'd melt the snow the instant I got off the lift.

"He told me he asked you to be his girlfriend. You said no because of Aiden?"

I didn't know what to say, so I just nodded.

Mom took a breath as if knowing she was about to say something awkward. "I know it's not my place to tell you who to date. But honey, Grayson has been so good for you. I think you should tell him yes."

"Oh my gosh, Mom! You did not just say that!"

I couldn't believe it. My own mother was playing matchmaker!

At my mortification, my mother became determined. "Having a boyfriend is a perfectly normal part of being a teenager, and I don't want you to miss out on such a special experience because of my mistakes." She stopped then and frowned at me. "Having a boyfriend is okay, but no sex while you're still in high school, do you hear me?"

"Agh!" I shrieked in horror and threw my hands over my ears. "We are not talking about this!"

"I'm serious. If he tries to take your clothes off, I will kill him. You tell him I said that."

"No! I will not tell him you said that! I'm not telling anyone we had this conversation! In fact, I'm forgetting we had this conversation! Agh!"

We hit the top of the mountain, and I have never been so grateful to be off a ski lift in my life. Tara and Grayson were waiting for us at the top. I blushed even worse the second Grayson smiled at me. My mom saw that smile and was probably interpreting it in a million different ways.

"Owen and Libby just took off down the mountain. I think they had some kind of bet going. Libby was saying that understanding angles and aerodynamics made her the superior jumper."

I shook my head. "She was probably just saying that stuff to freak him out. She is an awesome jumper, though. She grew up on the mountain because her dad's a professional snowboarder."

"No way!"

"It's true," my mom said. "We've been to a few of his competitions over the years."

When I heard my mom's voice, I cringed and grabbed Tara's hand. "Come on," I said desperately. "I'm ready to ski."

"Don't you want to wait for your other friends?"

"Pam and Chloe were right behind me. Grayson and Mom can wait for them."

I tugged Tara with me down the mountain. Of course it only occurred to me once I reached the bottom that the minute I ditched them my mom probably told Grayson what she said to make me so upset. If he said anything about it, I was going to die. LITERALLY DIE!

We stayed out on the mountain until dusk and then picked up a bunch of pizza on the way to the condo. We stuffed ourselves silly, and then after an embarrassing serenade to the tune of Happy Birthday over a huge, blazing red velvet cake, I was showered with a mound of presents.

Movie tickets from Owen. A membership to the Museum of Natural History from Mom. Sunglasses and earrings from Chloe. A pair of high-heeled boots from Pamela—she seemed dead set on adding a few inches to my height whenever possible. The science club went in together on the entire collection of MythBusters DVDs, complete with a Jamie and Adam bobble head set—so awesome!

Grayson handed me his gift last. I was instantly curious as to what he got me for my birthday. He'd given me something every year for as long as I could remember. When we were younger it was things like Play-Doh or Barbie dolls, which I'm sure his mother picked. When he was old enough to shop for himself, the gifts turned into things like fake mustache kits and fart machines. Somehow, this year, I didn't think he shopped for my gift at *Spencer's*.

I tore off the paper and laughed when I saw the purple and pink heart-covered diary with a lock on it. Then I looked closer. Grayson had written a title on the cover for me with black permanent marker. The journal was apparently called "Avery Shaw's Secret Grayson Kennedy Love Diary." Beneath the title in smaller letters it said, "Every gruesome, girly detail of Post Shower Avery and Grayson. (With lots of exclamation points, smiley faces, and hearts!!!!)"

I felt my eyebrows fly up, and when I looked at Grayson, his eyes twinkled. "I couldn't let that boring thing you call a journal be your only record of the Avery Shaw Experiment. It's missing all the good stuff!"

He pulled a tiny key from his pocket and unlocked the book. He flipped it open to show me that the first few pages were already filled.

"I figured you might need some help getting started, so I went ahead and wrote down some of your thoughts on a few of your favorite A.S.E. moments so far."

"*My* thoughts?"

Grayson's grin widened to dimple status. "That's right. I'm sure you'll find it extremely accurate. I specifically recall you going into some detail about my broad shoulders and eyes like the ocean as you sat across from me at dinner that first night. I had no idea you were so attracted to me, Aves."

I slapped my hands over my face and groaned, but secretly I treasured the gift. I eyed the inch-thick book and doubted there'd be enough pages to hold all the gruesome, girly details I planned to write in it.

"Okay, guys," Owen said. "Who's ready for the hot tub?"

Everyone started to scatter, cleaning up wrapping paper, pizza plates, and empty soda cans until Libby found another gift. "Hey, there's one more here."

I took it and looked at my mom.

She shook her head. "It's not from me."

I scanned the room and everyone shrugged. I examined the bag, but there was no name on it. "Who is this from?"

Nobody fessed up.

"Just open it," Brandon said impatiently.

For a brief moment I wondered if it was secretly from Aiden and he'd somehow talked someone into bringing it for him. My heart pounded in my chest as I tore away the tissue paper.

I pulled the gift from the bag and held it up before I knew exactly what it was. It turned out to be a scandalously skimpy, dark red bikini and a gorgeous white sarong to go with it.

Definitely not from Aiden.

"What is *this?*"

I was still gaping at the outfit in horror when Grayson said, "Why is everyone looking at *me?*"

I glanced up and, sure enough, all eyes were on him, each face full of accusation. Almost everyone was trying not to laugh, but my mother looked exasperated.

"It's not from me!" Grayson said with a pure mask of innocence.

Libby snorted. "Who else would it be from?"

"What? Just because I was the one who mentioned the hot tub and happen to know that Avery only owns lame one-pieces that look like they came from my grandma's closet, doesn't mean that *I* bought her the very tasteful swimwear that will probably look killer on her."

There was a beat of silence, and then the whole room exploded into laughter. It was so loud that we didn't notice the door to the condo burst open. At least not until Aiden ran in shouting my name, sounding half pissed off, half panicked.

Everyone was stunned into silence.

Aiden stumbled to a stop when he saw me. For a brief second there was a look of pure relief, and then he took in the scene. His eyes swept over everyone in the room and then noticed the half-eaten birthday cake.

Understanding finally hit him. "This is a birthday party? You're having a *birthday party?*"

I wasn't sure what he wanted me to say, and from the looks of it, no one in the room felt inclined to help me out. "Um…it *is* my birthday. What else would I be doing up here?"

Aiden looked shell shocked. "My mom said you and Grayson came up here today, and I just thought…"

Grayson walked up next to me. "You thought I brought her up here alone." He laughed one hard, humorless laugh.

"You thought I was going to try to get her to sleep with me?" He put his arm over my shoulder. He was so tense I wondered if he was using me to hold himself back from throwing punches. "I can't believe you thought I would do that to Avery."

Aiden glared at Grayson while I pieced together a realization of my own. "You came up here to stop me. Because you were so sure I'd just jump right into bed with him the minute he tried to seduce me."

Aiden looked away from me, shame all over his face. A pain I'd come to recognize as the feel of Aiden Kennedy breaking my heart settled in my chest.

"Can we go upstairs and talk in private please?"

"No, we can't."

My answer was sharp and came out of nowhere. I felt Grayson stiffen in surprise next to me. I put my arm around his waist—so glad he was there to help hold me up. I had this really strange feeling forming in the pit of my stomach. It wasn't my familiar panic, and that scared me.

"I can't believe you would think that about me," I said.

Aiden seemed to get angry. "Of course I was worried about you! I know my brother, Avery. He's the master and you're so...so..."

"I'm so *what?*"

My voice sounded strange. I wasn't sure what was going on with me.

Grayson must have realized something was off too, because the hand that he'd had over my shoulders was now gently rubbing my back in a slow, soothing manner.

"Innocent," Aiden said. "Inexperienced."

"And so you assumed that I would just give it up to your brother because he was the first guy who ever showed interest in me?"

"Red alert! Red Alert!" Brandon muttered somewhere to the left of me. "Stage five here we come."

I heard the chime of a video camera being turned on and Levi whispered, "Systems are a go. We are about to witness science in action. After weeks of no progress, A.S.E. test subject Avery Shaw is finally about to emerge from her guilt and experience the fifth stage of grief. Just as her lab partner predicted, it looks to be an explosive scene."

"Do you guys *mind?*" I snapped at them. I turned back to Aiden. "Do you think I'm that insecure?" I asked him in a tight voice. "That *desperate?*"

Aiden sighed. "It's not just that, Aves." He raked his hands through his hair in frustration. "You've been so vulnerable lately."

"Tell me he did not just say that," Libby said.

I think it was Owen who chuckled and replied, "She's going to tear him a new one."

I couldn't be bothered with the commentary. I felt my face turn red, and for the first time in my life, it wasn't because I was blushing.

"And why might I be feeling vulnerable lately, Aiden? Whose fault would that be?" Aiden flinched. "Not that it's any of your business, but Grayson hasn't been trying to take advantage of me. He's been bending over backwards to help me."

Aiden's hands clenched into fists. "Yeah, I saw how he was trying to help you."

That was it. I just snapped. "You have no idea what you saw! That kiss was a dumb science experiment! Grayson agreed to be my partner for the science fair after *you* quit on me!"

"An experiment?" Aiden scoffed. "What kind of experiment would require you to kiss somebody?"

I marched over to my backpack and yanked my science journal from it. We'd turned so many things into experiments that I'd taken to carrying the book with me everywhere. Without giving it a thought, I chucked the stupid thing right at Aiden's head.

"This one you jerk! I'm trying to find the stupid cure to a broken heart!"

My journal plastered him right in the face. He stumbled back, shocked. He picked up the book, leafed through a few pages, and then popped like a balloon—his anger completely gone.

He might have been finished yelling, but I was just getting started. "You *broke* me, Aiden! Not just my heart, but every single part of me! Grayson just happened to be there when I shattered and was kind enough to pick up the pieces. He's been there for me every step of the way! He's just trying to help me get over you!"

For a minute it was so silent that I think everyone in the room must have been holding their breath.

"Aves…" Aiden whispered in a strangled voice.

The intimacy in the way he said my name felt like

another stab wound. "Don't call me that!" I hissed. "Only people who really care about me can call me that!"

"Aves, I do care about you. You're my best fri—"

"Don't you dare say that! I am *not* your best friend! I have been *nothing* to you since winter break."

"That's not true."

"You cut me completely out of your life! You've barely spoken two words to me in weeks. You made me feel guilty for trying to support you. You forced me to sit away from my friends at lunch!"

"I did not! You left with Grayson!"

"Because you were going to ask me to leave! Weren't you!"

Aiden shrunk back like a puppy being scolded for chewing shoes.

I managed to lower my voice a little. "You couldn't even stand to be near me. I was your best friend for seventeen years, and just like that, you got a girlfriend and forgot all about me."

"No!" Aiden shook his head frantically. "I didn't, Aves. That's why I broke up with Mindy. We got in a huge fight after you came to my debate. She told me I had to choose, so I did. I chose *you* Avery."

It was everything I'd wanted to hear since he dumped me in almost this exact spot six weeks ago. Funny how now that he'd finally said it, it didn't make a bit of difference. "Doesn't matter," I said. "It's way too little, way, way, way too late."

"Aves, come on. Don't do this. I know I screwed up—I

screwed up huge—but we can get past it. I'll do whatever it takes to make it up to you. You're not nothing to me. You're *everything*. I was just so close to you that I couldn't see it."

And finally, my anger was gone too. I was done. Probably for the rest of my life.

"That's real sweet, Aiden," I said in a dead voice. "But you shouldn't have come here. I think it's upsetting Grayson, and you're kind of ruining my birthday party."

Aiden sucked in a breath, no doubt recognizing those words. They were more or less the same ones he'd said to me at his debate. Now he knew what it felt like.

"I'm sorry, Aiden, but I'd like you to leave please."

I recognized the look of a person's heart breaking. I'd never seen it from this perspective before, but I was familiar with it enough to know that's what was happening to Aiden right then.

He didn't say another word to anyone. He just got up and quietly left. The moment the door shut behind him, I graduated from stage five and spiraled straight on into depression.

depression

Grayson

I thought it would feel good to watch Avery finally tell off my brother, only that wasn't the case at all. In reality it sucked. He totally deserved it, and, yes, part of me was more than satisfied when she'd thrown the book at him—literally—but I knew it hurt her to do it, and *that* I didn't like watching.

The only way to describe Avery after her fight with Aiden was tired. I'd expected one of her stress attacks. I thought she'd break into hysteric sobs the minute he left, but she just seemed exhausted. She didn't shed a single tear.

I was proud of her for that.

Her body sagged against mine, and for one long minute she buried her face in my chest, soaking up my comfort while I held her. Just about the time I expected one of her anxiety attacks to take over, she pulled her face back just far enough to look up at me and asked, "You don't really expect me to wear that swimsuit, do you?"

I was shocked, but I felt the smile creep across my face. All this stuff we'd been doing really was helping her. There was no question. The old Avery wouldn't have been able to deal with this, especially not with a room full of people still watching her.

"Hell yes, I do," I answered. I'd paid good money for that swimsuit after all.

She sighed. "Fine. But if I do, will you *please* refrain from perverted comments at my expense? I know you're not very good at that, but I seriously cannot handle it right now. I just want to go have some fun with my friends tonight, and I won't be able to do that if you make me feel completely self-conscious."

It was a reasonable request. I wasn't sure I'd be capable of it, though. "I'll try my best."

When the girls all emerged in their swimsuits ten minutes later I about had a heart attack. Pamela was on the girl's soccer team and Chloe was on the dance squad. I knew from personal experience exactly how in shape they were. Aside from Chloe's lack of chest, they both had utterly perfect bodies. Pretty much every girl I'd ever dated did.

Then there was Avery. She wasn't like them. Her body

wasn't perfect. You'd never call her chubby, like Libby—who really didn't look too bad in the tasteful tankini she wore—but you wouldn't call her skinny like Tara, either. Poor Tara was so thin she looked like a sixth grader in her bathing suit.

Avery was what I would call soft. She had shape to her—waist, hips, a chest I've raved enough about already that I don't think you really need me to tell you exactly how perfect it looked tied up in that top—but you couldn't see every muscle beneath her skin. Nor were her bones showing. Add to that her flawless, cream-colored skin, and you got a very inviting, smooth, soft body that practically begged for you to sink your fingers into it.

Avery was something new for me. I wanted to know how a body like hers felt. I wanted to touch her. I wanted to explore every inch of her. I wanted it so bad that Owen chucked a towel at me with a meaningful look.

"Your weeks of celibacy are starting to show."

"It's not the celibacy that's doing it."

Owen looked over at the girls all gathering by the door. After a minute he said, "Little Miss Crazytown doesn't look as horrifying as I expected."

My eyebrows flew up at that, even though I'd just thought the same thing about Libby.

"Actually…" Owen chuckled. "Geek One and Geek Two over there are the sorest on the eyes. Twenty bucks says neither of them has ever kissed a girl before."

I followed his gaze to Brandon and Levi. Impossibly, they managed to fit the nerd stereotype even more perfectly in all their gangly glory. They had their shorts pulled up dangerously high on their waists, and Levi even had on prescription goggles.

No, I am not kidding. Prescription goggles.

They were elbowing each other and whispering as they both tried to discretely check out Pam and Chloe.

I laughed. "Same twenty says they'd both have asthma attacks if they ever got close enough to a girl to try it. Come on, dude, let's go. I need to hit the pool."

Owen smirked. "I hope for your sake the water's really cold."

Down at the pool the strangest thing happened. Once we were all in the water, Chloe dunked Owen and started a massive water fight. The weird part was, the fight instantly turned into boys versus girls, and somehow the lines of social status were blurred. For a while we weren't cool kids and geeks. We were all just friends of Avery having a good time. Never tell anyone I said this, but it was kind of cool. The science nerds can be pretty entertaining.

Eventually the girls raised the white flag and suggested we move the party to the hot tub. I squeezed in next to Avery, of course, and laughed when Libby pushed Brandon out of his spot in order to be by Owen. The fearful look on Owen's face was classic.

When everyone settled into the crowded space, the differences between the cliques slammed back into place. Before the silence could get awkward, I exaggerated a stretch and dropped my arm over Avery's shoulder. It got the laugh I hoped for.

"I know you said you weren't ready to be my girlfriend,

Aves, but would you still be my sweetheart?"

"What do you mean?"

The Valentine's dance was next weekend. No doubt Pamela and Chloe had been talking about it for at least two weeks, but being asked to a dance was so far off Avery's radar that she didn't recognize what I was doing.

I smiled at her confusion. "Will you be my date to the Sweetheart Dance next weekend?"

"Oh!" Avery gasped. Her eyes got really big, and her face flushed bright red. No doubt she was remembering our last dance and imagining what a whole night together could be like. I know I was. I wasn't sure I could survive that much torture, but I was looking forward to trying.

"Oh, um, actually Libby and I were going to go to the revival theater this weekend. They're doing a Nicholas Sparks movie marathon."

I didn't see how that was appealing, but before I could say so, Libby said, "No, it's okay. Go to the dance. I'll just make Brandon go with me."

"No way, Libby," Brandon immediately argued. "I can't subject myself to such rubbish."

"I'll let you put your arm around me in the theater," Libby negotiated.

"Will you let me feel your boob?"

"Are you serious?" Pamela asked, offended on Libby's behalf.

"You cannot ask a girl if you can touch her boob!" Chloe added, disgusted. "It's so degrading."

Owen and I both choked on laughs, but Libby ignored

Pam and Chloe. She took a moment to seriously consider it. "I won't rule out the possibility," she finally said. "There is a chance that with Ryan Gosling on the screen, I will be in the mood to make out."

"Fine. For that, I will sacrifice my manly dignity and suffer through some of the sappiest movies ever made."

Wow. There was no end to how much the nerds continued to surprise me. Owen, either, for that matter. He was staring at Libby like she was an unsolvable equation.

"There," I said, turning my attention back to Avery. "Libby's all taken care of."

"Yeah, sounds like she'll be in good hands." Owen snickered.

Libby grinned at Owen. "If you'd rather I be in your big, strong, capable hands instead, that can definitely be arranged. I wouldn't need Ryan to get me hot with you sitting next to me."

The nerds all snickered, as if this statement didn't shock them at all, but Pamela and Chloe gasped. Owen floundered for a moment and then snorted. "You are insane if you think I am ever going on a date with you."

Libby rolled her eyes. "Your loss. I happen to have the spirit of a wildcat. I could take you places sexually you never knew existed."

This time even the nerds gasped.

"Libby!" Avery cried.

"What? When a girl knows what she wants, she should go for it." Libby waved a hand at Owen. "Look at those abs! Libby definitely wants." She glanced up at Owen. "Can I feel them?"

"*What?*"

Libby didn't give Owen the chance to say no.

Owen was too shocked to stop her as she placed her hand on his chest and slowly dragged it down his six-pack. She let out this tiny squeak of excitement, which sent Owen scrambling from the hot tub so fast I wondered just how low her hand had gone.

"Whoa! Avery!" he yelled as he snatched up his towel. "Tell your crazy cat friend to stop objectifying me! I'm not a piece of meat!"

That sent Pamela and Chloe into peels of laughter. "Karma, Owen," Chloe gasped, clutching at her stomach from laughter. "Maybe next time you start to objectify a woman you'll think twice!"

After that, we all went back upstairs. I caught Avery's hand and linked our fingers together before she could take off ahead of me. "So?" I asked her. "You never gave me an answer. Will you go to the dance with me?"

"I'm sorry, Grayson, but I don't think I'm up for a Valentine's dance this year. Actually, I'm quite positive I want to forget the holiday entirely."

I was surprised she turned me down. She'd seemed okay all night. This was the first sign that she was struggling with what happened.

"You sure?" I asked. "I think we could have some fun despite everything with Aiden."

"I'm sure. Sorry. But I know you won't have a problem finding another date."

Sure. If I wanted another date. Which I didn't.

That was the beginning of an endless string of rejections from Avery. She didn't go to the dance with me. I tried several more times that week to get her to say yes and then just ended up going stag. On the actual day of February fourteenth, she wouldn't even answer any of my texts.

After that, she stopped coming to my basketball games and said no to hanging out on the weekends no matter what I suggested we do. Pulling the experiment card didn't even work anymore.

I'd never been more frustrated in my entire life. I got that she'd been through a lot and that she was trying to cope, but I was losing my patience. I could deal with her stupid mood swings and insecurity when she was trying to get past them, but she wasn't trying anymore. As adorable as I thought the girl was, her wallowing in self-pity was not attractive. Nor was it any fun to be around.

By March, I was so fed up I just stopped trying. For two weeks, I didn't see or talk to Avery outside of lunch and science club. I had way too much else on my plate anyway. The basketball team had made it all the way to the state championships, so we were holding extra practices. It was also the last week of third term, so all of my classes had major tests that week. It was a cruel twist of fate, really, and it left me absolutely no time or desire to deal with a mopey, depressed, cranky Avery. Especially not when she didn't want to hang out with me anyway.

I didn't really have time to think about Avery's current stage of grief. Depression was something I'd never understood. Anger and guilt made sense, but I'd never felt depression. I didn't get how someone could just be sad all the time.

I figured that when Avery was ready to get over it, she would. It didn't occur to me that she might be unable to pull herself out of it until her mom came to my house the morning after the state championship.

We'd lost the game, which was okay—second in the state is still awesome—but it was one of the biggest games of my life, and Avery had blown me off when I asked her to come. I honestly wasn't in the best mood that morning, and seeing Kaitlin sitting at my breakfast table only reminded me how much Avery's brush-off had hurt.

Kaitlin and my mom had made up, but she was still really mad at Aiden, so she hadn't been to the house as much.

I looked around for my mom, but there was nobody home.

"Morning, Kaitlin," I muttered awkwardly as I went in search of some juice.

"Afternoon," she corrected. There was a nervousness about her that didn't make sense.

"What's up? Where is everyone?"

"Your parents went to Home Depot. Something about re-tiling the upstairs bathroom?"

I rolled my eyes. My parents were obsessed with remodeling. Real Do-It-Yourselfers. A strange hobby, if you ask me, when they could afford to hire someone to do it for them.

"I haven't seen Aiden," she added.

Not surprising. "Not many do these days. He's been pretty pathetic since Avery's birthday."

Kaitlin suddenly sent me a desperate look. "I actually came to see you. I'm really worried about Avery."

"Don't know what I can do to help," I grumbled.

Kaitlin's face fell in disappointment. "I know you're frustrated, but try not to be too upset with her. Please. I need your help, Grayson."

She had my attention instantly. She'd been walked out on by her husband when Avery was four. She'd become quite the independent woman since then. Asking for help was something Kaitlin Shaw did not do.

"I know she's been sad and a little depressed lately, but I'm sure she'll be fine."

"It's more than a little," Kaitlin whispered. "She sleeps most of the day. She's losing weight because she's not eating. She failed her math test this week. Failed! Avery! Several of her teachers have called me, concerned about her. I tried to ask her about it, but she won't talk to me."

Kaitlin started to cry. "I think Avery has a serious problem. Libby's been over a couple times, but nothing seems to work."

I could hardly believe what Kaitlin was telling me. I'd known Avery was having a hard time, but none of that sounded like her. I couldn't imagine a world where Avery Shaw failed a test and blew off Libby. I knew she was blowing me off, but I figured that was just because of Aiden. It's what she did when she felt guilty. I suddenly felt awful for giving up on her.

Kaitlin's hand came down on top of mine. She was shaking. "Grayson," she whispered. "Please."

I was shocked at the swarm of emotions that swept through me right then. I think that one word caused me to go through my own stages of grief all at once. Shock, anger, depression, frustration, and even grim resignation overwhelmed me in mere seconds.

"I tried," I said. "I tried everything I could think of, but I can't help her. You should talk to Aiden." My voice dripped with bitterness.

Kaitlin gave me a heartbroken smile. "Don't give up on her now. She needs you."

It actually hurt to hear her say that. It hurt because I wanted it to be true, but it just wasn't. "She doesn't want my help! She wants Aiden! She's always wanted Aiden!" I took a breath. I shouldn't be yelling at Kaitlin. None of this was her fault.

Kaitlin shook her head furiously. "She loves you. I know she does."

I suddenly felt like I'd run a marathon. I was tired of trying. Tired of lying to myself and trying to make something true that wasn't. I couldn't do it anymore. Not even for Kaitlin. "She loves my brother. He doesn't deserve her, but if she really needs help, he's the one she'll listen to."

Aiden's voice startled both Kaitlin and me. "That's not true."

He walked into the kitchen looking pale and rumpled. He stuck a bowl and spoon in the sink and then turned to

Avery's mom. "Kaitlin," he said in a strangled voice. His eyes filled with tears, and he couldn't get any more words to come out of his mouth, but the "I'm sorry" was obvious.

I think Kaitlin wanted to be mad at him, but she couldn't do it with him looking so pathetic. "I'll forgive you if you forgive me," she said.

Aiden nodded miserably and then blushed as he tried to wipe away the evidence of his tears.

Kaitlin stood and gave Aiden a hug, then said she needed to go. As she walked out the door, she gave me one last pleading look. "Please don't give up on her. She needs help, Grayson. I'm trying, but no one has ever helped her as much as you did."

The door clicked shut, and I just sat there at the table, overwhelmed by Kaitlin's visit. I didn't want to let her down. If Avery really was that depressed, then I wanted to help, but I just didn't know what else I could do for her.

Aiden plopped down in a chair across the table from me and met my eyes. "Kaitlin's right about Avery."

I was surprised. Aiden and I hadn't exactly been on speaking terms for the last few months.

"You changed her," he admitted grudgingly. "At first I was so mad at you for it. One lunch with you and suddenly she looked different. She was hanging out with other people, going to basketball games and parties. It was like I didn't even recognize her, and I hated you for ruining her."

I realized I was grinding my teeth when my jaw started to hurt. "If she changed, it was only for the better."

Aiden looked down at his lap. "I know," he said quietly.

"You can hardly even notice her anxiety anymore. The old Avery never could have gone off on me the way she did on our birthday. She's stronger because of you. Healthier."

Aiden gulped, and his voice shook as he forced the next words from his mouth. "Until we fought at the condo, she was happier than I'd ever seen her in our whole lives. You did that."

I scoffed. "Yeah, right. If I made her so happy, then what happened? She's rejected me a thousand times over again and always for the same reason—you. She loves *you*."

"You are so blind."

"You have no right to call me blind when you missed her feelings for you for *seventeen years*." I felt my anger boiling up inside me. It pissed me off to hear him saying these things when I *knew* he was the one she wanted. "You better have been clueless, anyway, because I'd hate to think you realized what you were doing to her all those times you broke her heart."

Aiden glared at me, but he was just mad at himself for that one. "So we're both idiots," he said. "Doesn't mean she didn't fall in love with you."

I couldn't take it anymore. I flew to my feet so fast I sent the chair crashing to the floor behind me. "Everything we've ever done together has been about *you!*" I yelled, slamming my fists down on the table. "All the time we spent together was because of you! She didn't hang out with me because she wanted me. She was trying to get over you! I'm just a damn science fair partner to her!"

Aiden rose to his feet and met my volume with a shout

of his own. "Why do you think I went to the condo on her birthday? It wasn't because I thought she would sleep with just anyone. I knew she was in love with you, and I couldn't let you hurt her!"

He rolled his eyes when I glared at him. "Are you really going to blame me for thinking you could? How many countless girls have you made fall for you and then tossed away when you got bored with them?"

"I didn't mean to make them all fall for me," I said defensively.

Aiden shrugged. "They still fell. Every single one of them. Avery's no different."

I started to argue, but Aiden glared at me so hard I shut my mouth.

"You think I don't know her well enough to see it?" he hissed. "You've been her friend for two-and-a-half months. I've been her friend her whole life! I know everything about her. I know what she's going to do before she does it. I know what she actually means when she says something and she's just trying to be nice. I even know all of her different laughs and sighs. I know every single facial expression she has, and the way she looks at you? Trust me. Avery is crazy about you."

Aiden glared at me again like he was hoping I might explode into a pile of ash. I didn't think he could make me any madder, but he had some freaking nerve. "If that's true, why the hell should it piss you off?"

Aiden's face flushed deep red, and he came around the table to stand toe to toe with me. I was quite a bit taller than him, but it didn't stop him from getting right up in my face. "Because she should be mine!" Aiden screamed. "She *was* mine! Yeah, I really, really screwed up, but I could have fixed it. I knew by the end of school that first day that I'd made a mistake. I was going to dump Mindy and apologize, but you'd already swooped in like a damn vulture! Then you did what you always do."

"Excuse me?" I asked incredulously.

Aiden glared at me as if he loathed me more than was humanly possible. "Don't act like you didn't! You took her out. You made her popular. You kissed her. For a couple weeks you were perfect, caring, charming Grayson Kennedy until she fell for you. Then you got bored and dropped her like every other girl you've ever dated, and now she's so depressed, her mother was over here begging you to fix it!"

My vision went red. I threw my fist so fast Aiden never saw it coming. I hit him so hard he flew back and landed on his butt. He blinked up at me in shock, while blood ran down his face. I was sure I'd just broken his nose, but I was too furious to care.

"I didn't get bored and drop her, you asshole! I got rejected! I asked her to be my girlfriend, and she said no. She said it wouldn't be fair to me because she'd only be doing it hoping it would make her forget about you. She fed me some stupid line about how I deserved someone who could actually care about me, and that wasn't her."

Aiden stopped worrying about the blood running from his nose and gaped up at me. "*What?*"

"She loves you, you undeserving bastard. If anybody fell

for anybody in the last few months it was me."

I sank back into my chair at the table. Now I understood why Avery had seemed so tired after she exploded on Aiden. Being this angry was exhausting both physically and mentally.

"I love her, Aiden."

There it was. I'd been refusing to admit it for weeks, but there was no use denying it anymore.

"You…" Aiden's face paled, and I don't think it was from blood loss.

I shrugged helplessly. "She's depressed right now because of you. It started the night you busted in on her birthday. I tried for weeks to cheer her up. I tried everything I could think of, but nothing I did helped. She didn't want me. She never has."

My head hurt too bad to deal with this anymore. "I'm going back to bed."

acceptance

Avery

I knew as part of the grieving process I would get here eventually, but I hadn't meant to fall apart so badly. Depression runs in my family. I'd had problems with it before, and so I told myself I wouldn't let it overwhelm me. But that's the thing with depression. Sometimes there is no controlling it. Sometimes it sneaks up on you.

Obviously I'd known it was coming. I even realized when I said no to going to the dance with Grayson that I was starting to feel it, but suddenly I was so deep in it I didn't know which way was up anymore. In fact it was so bad I wondered if maybe I hadn't been feeling a bit depressed all along.

It was mid-March now. Over a month had already slipped by since my birthday. I'd barely noticed. I'd been too busy being sad to realize exactly how depressed I was until my mom woke me up one Saturday morning and forced me to go see someone.

After my counseling session—and after my mom filled the prescription of anti-depressants the doctor had prescribed for me—I wasn't in the mood to talk to my mother anymore. I went straight to my room and stayed there.

It was two in the afternoon when the weight of someone sitting down on my bed woke me.

"Avery?"

His quiet voice was so timid, but it was still one of my favorite sounds in the whole world. It was a voice I knew as well as my own.

"Aiden?" I sat up and almost screamed when I saw his face. "What happened to you?"

Aiden shrugged like it was no big deal. "I pissed off Grayson."

"*Grayson* did that to you? You're disfigured!"

Aiden winced. "I *really* pissed him off."

I hated to be so startled, but Aiden looked awful. Half his face was black and blue and his nose was swollen to twice its normal size. I couldn't believe Grayson had hit him.

"Is your nose broken?"

"Not badly. Doctor said it would heal on its own."

Once the subject of his bruises was out of the way, I

wasn't sure what else to say. I didn't know what he was doing in my room, and I wasn't sure if I wanted him there. Things got awkward, fast.

Outside, a dog barked, snapping us both from the thick silence that had settled between us. Aiden pulled his thoughts together and said, "Come with me to the Natural History Museum. My parents got me an annual pass for my birthday. I haven't used it yet."

It figured. "My mom got me a pass too."

"I know. They thought we'd like to be able to go together."

I couldn't make sense of my emotions. I was feeling a whole spectrum of them. In that moment bitterness won out. "Must have bought them a long time ago."

Aiden stood up and started pacing my small bedroom at the foot of my bed. "Actually, I suggested them for both of us a week before our birthdays," he explained. "When my parents gave me mine that afternoon, I was going to come see if you would go with me, just the two of us."

I'm not sure why that was so painful to know, but I had to close my eyes and push back tears. Then I figured something out. "That's when your parents told you I'd gone up to the condo with Grayson."

Aiden obviously didn't want to go there. He stopped pacing and caught my eyes in an unyielding stare. "Come to the museum with me."

I wanted to go with him. As much as I was mad at him, I could never hate him. He must have known that, or he wouldn't be here. I missed him so much, but I was scared of him now, so I chickened out. "I don't feel like going to the museum today."

"I know you don't feel like it. You haven't felt like doing anything for weeks. I'm asking you to come anyway. I'll beg if I have to."

"No."

"Why?" Aiden demanded. "Because you're depressed? Because you hate me? Because you want to get back at me?"

All of his reasons probably applied, but they weren't what was stopping me. I shook my head, but his eyes demanded an answer.

"Because I'm scared of you. I don't trust you not to hurt me again."

Aiden stopped pacing, devastated by my confession. He walked over to the window and stared out of it. I could barely hear him when he said, "I deserve that."

We lapsed into another long silence.

Aiden noticed my new diary on my desk and, after reading the front cover, held it up to me with a questioning look.

I felt myself blush. "He gave me that for my birthday," I muttered. "It's a long story."

Aiden set the book back down without saying anything and then looked at the large corkboard collage that now hung on the wall above my desk. It was the only thing that had changed about my room since the last time Aiden had been in here. It started out as an outline for the experiment, but then as Grayson and I began to go places and do things, it became more of a collection of souvenirs.

It had everything from a printout of our bowling scores to the tabs from our Red Bull cans glued onto an index card in the shape of a heart. And there were endless pictures. Pictures taken during science club and from Grayson's basketball games. There were tons from the party and my birthday and a few of my favorite random ones of Grayson and me together.

Aiden had his back to me, so I couldn't study his face as he looked at the collage, but watching him examine it made me feel bad. I'd done so much without him. Looking at that board, he probably thought I was a completely different person.

"I was planning to use it as a visual aid at the science fair. Just kind of a fun backdrop to all of the actual pieces of the display, but now it looks like I won't need it. The Avery Shaw Experiment had been put on hold, most likely indefinitely."

Aiden finally turned around and looked at me. He sounded cautious as he said, "Why?"

I shrugged. "The science fair is next weekend. I don't think there's any way to finish in time. I don't know how to reach the last stage of grief, and I think my partner has given up on me."

Aiden reached up to touch his bruised face and muttered, "My nose would have to disagree."

Before I could ask him why Grayson hit him—I suspected I was the cause of their fight—he asked, "What is the final stage of grief?"

I felt myself blush again. "Acceptance," I whispered,

looking down at my lap. "Hope."

Aiden didn't say anything.

When I finally looked up, he was watching me. He was chewing on his top lip as if debating whether or not to say what was on his mind. He always did that when he was nervous.

"What?" I asked.

He pushed his hand through his hair and then sat down on my bed again. "Maybe you've just been looking for the answer to this one in the wrong place."

I didn't want to tell him I hadn't been looking for the answer at all. I'd given up weeks ago. But right now he had me interested.

Aiden knew me too well. He knew that playing to my analytical nature would work better than graveling or bribing or anything else he could come up with. He was "playing the science card" as Grayson called it, because he knew I wouldn't be able to resist that.

"What do you mean?" I asked slowly.

Aiden smiled at his victory.

"People who lose their loved ones often visit gravesites," he said. "They talk to the dead. They get all their feelings off their chest in order to make peace. You haven't done that."

Hadn't I? Was he forgetting what happened on our birthday? I think I unloaded quite a bit of my feelings that day.

Aiden knew exactly what I was thinking. "You yelled at me," he said. When I opened my mouth he quickly cut me off. "You had every right to do that. I don't blame you for it, but maybe you have things you want to say now that you're not so mad."

"I don't know what there is to say, but I am still confused," I admitted.

"Then give me the chance to explain. Ask me whatever you need to. I promise I'll answer anything you can throw at me as best I can. Let me try to apologize too. I can't ever erase what happened, but I can definitely try to make it up to you. Come to the museum with me today. Let me stand in for Grayson on this one. Let me help you find your acceptance."

My heart pounded at its first glimpse of hope in months. Was there really a chance I could find acceptance? Aiden's theory made sense. Facing the cause of your grief is necessary in order to obtain acceptance. How could I ever get closure without ever trying to make sense of what had happened?

I couldn't believe I hadn't realized this yet. I'd been trying so hard to push Aiden under the rug and forget him, but people don't forget the loved ones they lose. They make peace with them being gone. In order for me to get over my broken heart, I had to make peace with the person who broke it.

"Okay," I said. "Let's do it. Let's go to the museum."

We didn't say much on the hour-and-a-half drive to Salt Lake City. I think we'd just automatically come to some sort of silent agreement that the following discussion should wait until we were walking through the exhibits of the Natural History Museum. Friendly ground and all that. We were both at home in any museum. Washington DC was our Graceland.

Being there with Aiden was as familiar as it always was, and yet it was different now too. It was strained and slightly awkward in a way it never had been with us ever in our lives. It wasn't just the unresolved issues. We had both changed over the last few months.

We were well into an exhibit on the history of ancient civilizations when we finally started to talk. We were standing in front of a display of Zallinger's *March of Progress* when Aiden brought it up. He looked at the figure of the Modern Man and sighed.

"You know what I think it was?" he asked. At first I didn't know what he was talking about. He pointed at the statue and said, "This is you. You are fully evolved. I'm still just here..." He walked over to the next figure down the line—a statue of good old Cro-Magnon Man.

Somehow I managed not to smile. I studied the less-evolved human a moment and then pushed Aiden a little further down the line. Neanderthal Man was tempting, but I walked him all the way back to Homo Erectus.

He looked at the hunched over figure, who was almost more ape than human, and frowned. I don't know what his problem was. It seemed about right to me.

"I don't even merit early Homo Sapiens?"

"I thought this was generous," I said dryly.

Aiden tried to be offended, but he ended up smiling. He looked at me a second too long. "I miss you, Aves."

His smile widened, but the fact that he missed me hurt.

I had to start walking again.

"Avery."

Aiden grabbed my hand and pulled me to a stop. "It's the truth, Aves. I miss you like crazy."

When he didn't let go of my fingers right away, I jerked back and folded my arms. "Why'd you stop talking to me?" I tried to keep the hurt out of my voice, but my eyes welled up, giving me away. "I don't understand what I did to make you hate me."

Aiden started to reach out to me but stopped himself and shoved his hands in his pockets. "I never hated you. I was never even mad at you."

"Then what happened?"

Aiden sighed. He glanced around us. "Dinosaur bones?"

I nodded, and he tentatively held his hand out as if he wanted me to take it.

Nervous energy spiked through me.

"Come on, Aves." He curled his fingers up in a "give me" gesture.

I didn't know what else to do, so I placed my hand in his. Aiden wrapped his fingers around mine gently and then smiled at me. I felt my face get hot, so I looked at the ground.

Aiden began to walk with me across the museum. I concentrated on our hands, swinging loosely in the space between us, and tried not to freak out. I had more questions now than I did before. I knew this was something boys do— Grayson took my hand pretty much every time we walked anywhere together, and sometimes he held it when we were driving—but Aiden had never acted like this before.

"I didn't mean to hurt you, Aves. I was really confused. The way we were raised was…"

His voice trailed off when he couldn't find the right word for it. I would have supplied something, but I didn't know how to describe it either.

"Do you remember when your dad split and you and your mom lived with us for a couple months? I remember crying every night for weeks after you guys got your own place. I didn't understand why you had to leave."

I smiled at the story, but it made me sad too. I had my own set of memories from then. First I lost my dad, but Aiden was there and made it okay, but then we left him too. It took me a long time to understand why.

"Growing up the way we did," Aiden said. "It was like I had a twin sister who lived a mile away. You're my best friend. You always have been, but it's like we never had a choice about that."

My lungs tightened in my chest. He felt forced into being my best friend?

"I'm sorry."

"I never minded, Avery. I couldn't have asked for a better best friend. When I started talking to Mindy, all the sudden nothing made sense anymore. I liked her. I'd never really liked anyone before because I always had you. But I didn't like you the same way I liked her."

I tried to ignore the sinking feeling in my stomach. "You liked me like a sister."

Aiden shook his head. "I always knew you weren't really

my twin sister, but I didn't know exactly what you were to me, either. Does that make sense?"

"Yeah, I guess. But why didn't you ever tell me? You were in that class with Mindy all semester, and you never mentioned her even once."

Aiden sighed, and his pace slowed to almost a stop. People in the museum weaved around us. "I think that was my first mistake. When I got partnered with Mindy at the beginning of the semester, she helped me a lot with my speeches for class." He shrugged. "I liked giving the speeches. It was fun and I was good at it, and I liked Mindy because she was different. I didn't tell you because it was the first thing I'd ever done on my own. You and I did everything together. This was something that I could do by myself. I'd never needed that, but once I had it, I really liked it."

Aiden stopped in front of a large dinosaur display and raked his free hand through his hair. "We did so much together that it was like I wasn't my own person. I didn't know how to separate us. I didn't know who I was without you. I needed something that was mine, you know? Mindy and debate did that for me. I was afraid that if I told you about them, I would lose that feeling."

I glanced up at Aiden. He was staring at the dinosaur but not really paying attention to it. As I looked closely, I could see how strung out he was. I hadn't noticed it before because of the bruises covering his face, but he looked tired and stressed. His eyes and cheeks seemed a little sunken in as if he'd lost some weight recently. He was pale and his hair needed a cut. He hadn't been his normal self for a while.

In that moment I realized that Aiden needed my acceptance as much as I did. We weren't meant to be apart. Maybe we weren't meant to be together the way I'd always imagined, but we couldn't spend the rest of our lives avoiding each other, either.

I gave his hand a small squeeze. "I would have understood. I would have given you all the space you needed."

Aiden squeezed my hand back and tugged me closer to him. "I should have realized that," he said with a sigh. "I'm really sorry, Aves."

I shrugged. "It's okay. I was never really upset about that anyway. I just didn't understand why you wouldn't even talk to me anymore." My eyes started burning again. "It was like you hated me. You were my best friend. You were the person I loved most and trusted most in the whole world, and all of a sudden you weren't a part of my life anymore."

I pulled my hand from Aiden's in order to wipe the tears that gathered in my eyes. I walked down a little ways to a drinking fountain and gulped down some water. I even splashed a little on my face. It helped ease a bit of the panic. I sat down on a bench and attempted to get my emotions under control again.

Aiden sat down, leaving a foot of space between us like he wasn't sure I wanted him near me.

"It was the same for me, you know," I said, sniffling. "I didn't know who I was without you, either. I don't think there was a part of me that didn't include you. When you abandoned me, it was like half of myself was just gone. First my dad left me, and then you. I didn't even know how to breathe anymore. If Grayson hadn't been there to hold me together, I don't know what would have happened."

So much for gaining control of my emotions. I started to cry, and Aiden's arms came around me. I turned into his shoulder and clung go him. Then I lost all control and started to sob. "How could you do that to me?" I cried.

I'd never felt so raw in all my life as when I pulled the bandage off my damaged heart for Aiden right then. I'd been trying to suppress my feelings for so long, trying to be strong, but as I sat there with him, I opened myself up and shared all of my hurt with him.

Aiden tightened his grip on me, but the hug wasn't exactly right. He's so much closer to my size. His arms didn't engulf me the way I was used to.

I breathed in deeply. My nose was filled with the smell of the soap Aiden uses and a hint of his peppermint gum, but I wasn't settled the way I was expecting. He was missing a certain hint of sweet and spice. It took me a moment to realize I was missing the smell of Grayson's cologne.

"Why don't we go outside and get some fresh air?" Aiden suggested and then led me out of the building.

We didn't say another word until we were outside and walking around the grounds of the museum. There was a layer of old snow on the ground, but the sun was shining and the fresh air was nice.

"I'm so sorry, Avery," Aiden eventually whispered. "I don't think I'll ever forgive myself for hurting you the way I did. I messed up so bad."

"What happened? If you weren't mad at me, why'd

things change so much? You said we would still be friends, but we weren't."

"It was because of Mindy. She was so threatened by you. When we got together, she asked me about you." Aiden shot me a grim smile. "Probably didn't handle that conversation very well, either. I told her I loved you more than anyone else on the planet. She didn't take that very well, so I tried to explain how it was for us. Hearing about how we grew up only made it worse."

I focused on the snow crunching under my feet as I listened to Aiden tell his story.

"I was determined to keep both relationships. You were my best friend, and Mindy was my girlfriend. There wasn't anything wrong with that. I should have been able to have both, but that first day back at school when Mindy and I were officially a couple at school, so many people were so shocked. Everyone we saw asked about you. Mindy couldn't handle it. She got angry and went off about how people didn't have relationships like ours. She said our moms were wrong to force us on each other."

Aiden got really quiet for a minute and then muttered, "She said a lot of stuff. She was captain of the debate team. She had a convincing argument. Plus, she was my first girlfriend. I'd never had anyone like me that way before. I wanted to make her happy."

"I get it," I said. I did understand to an extent, but it didn't explain the malice I sometimes felt. "But why did you seem so angry? Sometimes you'd look at me, and I would swear you hated me. What did I do wrong?"

Aiden's jaw clenched tight enough that he winced because it hurt his broken nose. That anger was exactly what I was talking about. He said I hadn't done anything wrong, but something was definitely bothering him.

"That wasn't you. I was mad at Grayson."

"Grayson?" The answer startled me. "Why?"

"Because it was so unlike him to take such an interest in you. I thought he was trying to take advantage of you. I was worried he was going to play you like he did every other girl, and…" He hesitated, shoving his hands in his pockets. "And because I was jealous."

I stopped walking and gawked at him. "Jealous? Why? You weren't interested in me. You had a girlfriend."

We'd come to the edge of a small pond. The edges were iced over. We stopped and Aiden kicked a chunk of ice. "Because I'm selfish," he said. "When you told me that you loved me and wanted to be with me, I hated that I was hurting you, but I was flattered at the same time."

I felt like I was going to die from embarrassment any moment. I actually expected myself to drop dead right there.

"I'd never thought about us like that before," Aiden said. "But after you mentioned it, I kept wondering. I knew almost immediately that I'd rather be with you than Mindy. I was going to break up with her right away, but it was too late. Grayson had already stolen you from me. You guys spent all your time together. He made you laugh and held your hand. I could see how much he made you happy, and I hated him for it."

My heart hurt again. It hurt for both of us. It hurt for

Grayson too. He was innocent in all of this.

"Please don't hate him for that. Grayson has done so much for me. He's one of my closest friends now."

Aiden tensed again. "I know." He shook his head in disgust. "And I drove you to him. I hurt you so bad that you needed him. I'm grateful he was there for you, but Aves, when I saw him kissing you, I almost killed him."

"Why?"

"Because I wanted it to be me."

"You what?" I gasped.

"I still want it to be me."

Aiden took my hand again and wet his lips as he pinned me with an intense gaze. "You asked me to kiss you once, and now I'm asking you, will you give me a second chance?"

I froze. And not because it was cold outside. For a second I convinced myself I was still in bed asleep. I'd wanted Aiden to kiss me for so many years, and now here he was asking to make that dream come true.

There was a part of me that wanted to say no—a piece of my brain, or maybe my heart that didn't want to kiss anyone but Grayson. But this was Aiden. I had to know. I owed it to myself to see what would happen. In more ways than one, I needed this.

"Okay," I whispered.

"Okay," Aiden answered. He took my other hand and stepped closer to me so that the tips of our shoes were touching.

He didn't kiss me right away. He swallowed and wet his lips again. He was as nervous as I was.

My pulse skyrocketed, and I couldn't keep any air in my lungs. I think I may have even been trembling a little when he finally leaned in.

He moved slowly, and I kept pretty still because I was scared of bumping his nose and hurting him. His kiss was shy at first as if he were testing the waters, and then his hand came up to my face, and he pulled me closer, urging my lips to part.

I liked kissing Aiden. He was sweet and considerate, and I could feel that when he pulled away, he wasn't quite ready to let the kiss end. It was a good kiss, but that was it. This kiss was all of the anticipation but none of the excitement that I got when I kissed Grayson. There was no spark. At least not for me.

Aiden looked happy until he saw my forced smile, and then his grin faded. "It's not going to happen, is it?" It didn't sound like he needed an answer.

"It was nice," I said.

"But it wasn't like kissing Grayson."

I felt my face go from polite to pained. The whole situation was so surreal. Who knew I'd ever be the one rejecting Aiden?

Aiden shook his head as if to let me know he wasn't upset. "I had to try, but I think I knew it was coming." He sighed. "As if I could ever compete with Grayson when he got all the looks and the charm."

I felt awful and tried to lighten the situation. "But you got all the brains, so he may be the one to rule the country someday, but you'll own it."

Aiden forced his mouth to curve up, and he squeezed my hand again.

"I'm sorry," I said.

"I'll survive." My heart sank a little more until he said, "As long as you forgive me and promise to always be my best friend."

It was that request that broke through the dark clouds in my world and brought me fully into the final stage of grief. If I were in a Disney movie, flowers would have bloomed and the birds would have started chirping.

Whether it was acceptance or hope or both, I knew that Aiden and I still loved each other. Things might be a little different between us now—no one heals without scars—but we were going to be okay. And if we could make it through this, we'd make it through anything.

Maybe now our relationship would be a healthy one. Maybe now we'd be able to have lives separate from one another and still be a part of each other. Maybe all of this needed to happen.

"I can do that," I said.

"And you're never allowed to have a birthday party without me ever again."

I laughed. "Promise."

Aiden let out a huge sigh of relief and leaned over to grab me up in a big hug. We held on tight, neither of us wanting to be the first to let go.

"Can you really forgive me?" Aiden asked, his voice thick with emotion.

I sniffled, but laughed at the same time. "I really can. I

do."

"I love you, Aves."

"I love you too, Aiden."

As we walked back to the car, I thought about how much my life had changed in the last few months. For the first time in what felt like forever, I was excited by the prospect of my future. With Aiden back, it was like I now had the best of both worlds.

"Are you going to be mad if I keep sitting with Grayson at lunch? It's the only time I ever see him at school."

Aiden sighed again, but it was playful. "It's okay. I get it."

"I'll rejoin you guys next year after he graduates," I promised.

Aiden watched me a minute with a frown on his face.

"What now?"

"I will never get used to the idea of you dating my brother. It's seriously disgusting. If you guys start making out in front of me all the time, I am going to need therapy."

I think I turned redder than I ever had before, and I felt a weight settle on my chest. "I think it might be too late for that," I said, unable to hide my disappointment. "I think Grayson's given up on me—not that I blame him."

Aiden rolled his eyes and shook his head. "If that were the case, I'd be able to smell right now. Trust me, Aves, he's still crazy about you. All you have to do is let him know you like him too."

hope

Grayson

I'm not going to lie, punching Aiden in the face felt really good. I hadn't meant to break his nose, but I didn't feel sorry for it either. Not even when I got grounded.

I don't think my mom actually wanted to ground me—I think she knew Aiden deserved what he got—but it's not like she could condone violence, so I received a month of house arrest. No friends over and no leaving the house for anything except family- or school-related activities, which, now that basketball was over, pretty much meant science club meetings. Oh freaking joy.

At least when I told Owen about it—I'd come clean to him about having to join science club—he offered to tough it out with me. I was a little shocked, but I wasn't going to complain.

"What kind of geek stuff do you guys do?" he asked as we wandered into Mr. Walden's classroom after school.

"Well, usually we work on our experiments for the science fair."

"Dude. Do you seriously have to go to that?"

"Unfortunately. But it really hasn't been that bad. Mine and Avery's experiment mostly consisted of me taking her on dates. For that, I got extra credit *and* didn't get kicked off the basketball team. One time I even had to kiss her as part of the experiment."

"You got extra credit for kissing?"

"Pretty much."

"You're shitting me."

"I believe those were Grayson's exact words when he learned about the experiment," Mr. Walden said as he came in the classroom with his standard cup of coffee. "Ones that almost earned him detention."

I laughed as Owen's face went pale. "Sorry, Mr. Walden!"

"Don't let me hear anymore of that language, Mr. Jackson."

"I won't."

Mr. Walden sighed but then smiled at me as he sat down. Actually, Mr. Walden is a pretty cool teacher.

"How is your experiment coming along, Grayson?"

The question made me want to be sick. Avery and I had worked so hard these last few months, and it was all for nothing.

I fell into a chair near Mr. Walden's desk and frowned at him. "We tried everything we could think of, and Avery's just not better. We were wrong. She's, like, broken forever or something, so I guess we failed the experiment."

Mr. Walden's face fell. "That's not your fault," he said.

He must have seen the guilt in my expression, because he got up from his desk and put a hand on my shoulder.

"It's nothing that you did, Grayson, and you couldn't have prevented it. You have been wonderful with Avery. Don't blame yourself, and don't blame your experiment."

"But I gave up on her. I was so frustrated. I didn't know she was really sick. Her mom made her see a doctor."

"She'll be fine. She's getting the help she needs now." He gave my shoulder one last squeeze before going back to his desk. "I bet she could really use a friend right now, though. It's not too late for you to help her get through her depression."

Mr. Walden was wrong. It *was* too late for me. I'd called her house Saturday night after her mom came to see me, but she was out with Aiden. Her mother told me he'd dragged her to the museum. I wanted to break his nose all over again. I told the jerk I was in love with her, and he turned around and took her on a freaking date.

It was my own fault. I knew he wanted her, and I was the one that told him how much she was still in love with him. Of course he went to her. I would have done the same thing if I thought I had a chance with her.

"Maybe she will get better," I said. "But if she does, it'll be because of therapy and medication, not the seven stages of grief. We were both wrong."

"Don't get discouraged, Grayson. Trial and error is a big part of science."

"Whatever." I didn't really want a bunch of teacher mumbo jumbo right then.

Mr. Walden sat there looking at me like I'd just told him I was dropping out of school to make a living selling drugs or something. He seemed sad, and for the first time in my life, I hated that I'd disappointed one of my teachers.

"I'm sorry I let you down, Mr. Walden," I mumbled. I felt the back of my neck get warm and reached up to rub it before Owen noticed my embarrassment. "I really did try, though. I swear! I told you I wasn't good at all this science stuff."

Mr. Walden's face went from sad to shocked. "Is that what you think? That you've failed and you've let me down?"

I shrugged uneasily. "Well, we did. The experiment was a bust. What happens now anyway? Do we get kicked out of the science fair? I suppose I don't get my extra credit, either, right?"

Mr. Walden jerked back in surprise, nearly spilling his coffee all over his desk. "Good hell, Grayson!"

I was surprised to hear the curse after all his lectures on the subject of foul language. Owen seemed pretty stunned too.

"Of course you'll get the credit!" Mr. Walden said. "You

did the work, didn't you?"

"Yeah, but we can't go to the science fair now."

"Why not?"

"Because we don't have a finished experiment. We failed!"

Mr. Walden sighed. "Do you know how many times Thomas Edison failed before he had a working lightbulb?"

"Uh…no?" Why would I know something like that?

"They say it was over a thousand, Mr. Kennedy."

"No way!" Owen said.

Mr. Walden smiled. "Indeed. Allegedly when he was asked about it, he said, 'I have not failed one thousand times. I have successfully discovered one thousand ways to *not* make a lightbulb.' Failure is a part of the process, Grayson. Of course you can still take your experiment to the fair this weekend. Yours will not be the only unsuccessful project there, and you may even still place."

"What? How?"

"The project itself is intriguing. I believe people will be fascinated with your efforts despite the negative outcome. All you have left to do is write up your conclusions, and you will be ready for Saturday."

Showing off a lame failed experiment didn't sound like much fun to me. "Maybe we still shouldn't go, though. The nerds are already embarrassed having to take a dumb jock like me to the fair with them. This experiment just proves them right. I don't want to ruin their day when they've all worked so hard."

Suddenly Mr. Walden had the look on his face that he

always had when he was about to start doling out the detention slips. "You are not a dumb jock, Grayson."

"Right." I scoffed.

Mr. Walden leaned back in his chair and rubbed his head like it hurt. I knew I exhausted the guy on occasion, but I thought we were past me giving him migraines.

He sighed and pulled his grade book out of his desk. He walked over and plopped it in front of me. After finding my name on his class list, he ran his finger down the line and stopped it on a B.

I was a little shocked. "Is that the grade from my test last week? Did I seriously pull a B?"

"No," Mr. Walden said gruffly. He scooted his finger back to a different column. This time he pointed at an A minus. "This was the grade you got on the test last week. The B is the grade you will see on your report card for third quarter when they're handed out this Friday."

Scratch being a little shocked. If I hadn't been sitting, I'd have fallen over in a dead faint. "You're totally shitting me, Mr. Walden!"

Mr. Walden frowned at me, but before I could apologize, he cracked a smile and said, "I assure you I am not *shitting* you, Grayson."

There was a round of laughter in the room. I hadn't realized that the science club geeks were all standing behind us, listening to the conversation.

Mr. Walden smiled at everyone and then met my eyes again. This time his were shining. I couldn't believe it, but the man was proud of me.

"I haven't added in the extra points from the science experiment yet, Grayson. This lift in your grade is purely from you actually turning in your homework assignments and studying for your tests. If you attend the science fair this weekend as we agreed on, and if you continue to apply yourself as you have been, I have no doubt you will graduate with an A in my class."

At that everyone broke out into a round of clapping and cheers. I took an exaggerated bow, pretending like it was no big deal, but it actually felt kind of awesome knowing I'd done so much all by myself. Well, it wasn't completely on my own. I totally owed the science squad.

"I think this calls for a celebration. What do you guys say to some applied physics for science club today? My treat."

"Applied physics?" Owen asked.

Now I understood why everyone laughed at me the first time I'd heard that term. The horror in Owen's voice was hilarious.

I slung my arm over his shoulder. "Don't worry. It's not as scary as it sounds."

"Sounds like a party in here."

Avery's quiet voice broke the scene like a sledgehammer through a window. She stood in the doorway to the classroom, blushing from the way she'd brought everything to a stop. She'd been so nonresponsive lately that she'd faded into the background both at lunch and here in science club. We weren't used to her speaking up anymore, and I wasn't the only one surprised when she'd interrupted the conversation.

Of course, we were also shocked because of who she'd dragged with her to science club.

Libby was the first to snap out of it and answer her. "It is," she said. "Today a miracle has occurred, and we are celebrating."

"Miracle?" I laughed. "Gee thanks, Lib."

"Grayson's going to get an A in physics!" Tara blurted, then promptly turned bright red.

"An *A*?" Aiden gasped. I rather enjoyed his shock. Jerk.

Avery wasn't shocked. Actually, she shocked me when she said "I'm not surprised," and her face lit up with a bright smile. I hadn't seen her smile like that since her birthday. It made my stomach get all fluttery. I had to look away from her before I blushed like some stupid tween experiencing his first crush.

"It's not a sure thing," I mumbled, looking anywhere but her eyes. "We still have to finish our project before the science fair this weekend."

"Well, then it's definitely a sure thing."

Surprised by the excitement in Avery's voice, I looked up and found her beaming at me. "We're done!" she squealed. "I've reached the final stage!"

I didn't know what to say. My eyes fell to her and Aiden's clasped hands. Whatever happened between them at the museum on Saturday obviously went well enough to pull her out of her depression and find acceptance.

I wasn't sure it counted as acceptance if she simply got what she'd wanted in the first place. Did she really get past the heartbreak, or did he just un-break it when he asked her out? There was a difference. But she looked so happy, and she'd clearly forgiven him for everything he did to her, so I didn't point that out.

I swallowed back bile and forced myself to smile at her. "That's great, Aves. I guess we have more than one reason to celebrate today then, huh?"

Avery nodded enthusiastically. Then she glanced at Aiden, and her smile died as if she'd just remembered my brother and I were not exactly getting along right now. She mustered up her courage and then asked the entire group, "Do you mind if Aiden comes with us? Debate is over, and I've been trying to convince him to come back to science club for the rest of the year."

I felt everyone's eyes turn to me, waiting to see what I thought so they could follow my lead. I was surprisingly touched to have earned the geek squad's loyalty.

I wanted to say no. Aiden didn't deserve to be welcomed back with open arms when he'd abandoned everyone in this room. I also wanted to tell him to get lost because I couldn't stand the sight of him and Avery together. I'd told myself this was coming, but seeing them standing so close to one another with their hands woven together was way harder to stomach than I'd anticipated. I wasn't sure I could survive them being a couple, but I had to find a way because Avery needed someone right now, and as much as I hated it, that someone obviously wasn't me.

"Sure," I forced myself to say. "If he wants to come."

Avery asked me to ride in Brandon's van with her, but I hopped in Owen's car with Libby and Tara. Was I avoiding them? Hell yes. I needed the ride to mentally prepare before I had to spend time with Avery and Aiden, The Couple.

At least no one else seemed to be having such a hard time with Aiden's presence. It helped keep the awkwardness to a minimum. Everyone was laughing and joking around as we all laced up our shoes.

"So you geeks want to explain to me how bowling is physics?" Owen asked.

Everyone laughed and Levi started spouting off words like velocity and inertia until Brandon interrupted. "No! No physics today. This is a celebration. Today we just play and have fun."

"I get Avery, Grayson, and Owen on my team," Levi said. "Losers buy the pizza!"

Libby stopped entering names into the computer and said, "No way. It's boys against girls. Winners get to kiss a boy of their choice."

"But I don't kiss boys," Owen argued.

Libby rolled her eyes at him. "Duh. But you won't be winning, so it doesn't matter."

I smiled to myself, feeling a "friendly wager" coming on. "Whatever the stakes, it can't be pizza. That's on me today. I really do owe you guys for my grade."

"Hey, yeah. Speaking of that, do you guys do math at all or just science?" Owen asked. "I'm getting a D in calculus."

Brandon sighed—probably because Owen looked like another dimwitted jock living up to the stereotype.

"Libby tutors calculus," Levi offered.

I snorted. It had to be Libby.

Owen cringed. "Does anybody *else* tutor math?"

Everyone laughed, and the game got started while I went to order the pizzas.

Just as I finished paying, someone walked up behind me. I knew without looking who it was. Besides the fruity smell that always followed her everywhere—today it was a tart apple smell—I could just feel it. I could feel her. My body was aware of hers on some sort of chemical level. Is that even possible? Someone should do a science experiment on that.

I knew Avery well enough to recognize that her tiny voice was on the verge of breaking when she said, "I'm sorry, Grayson."

I took a second to slam a poker face into place before I turned around. "It's okay," I lied. "I just want you to be happy." Well, that much was true anyway. I did want her to be happy. I just wanted to be the one who made her happy. "We've all been worried about you, Aves."

Avery cast her eyes down in shame. "I know. I'm sorry I let things get so out of hand."

"That wasn't really your fault."

Avery clearly disagreed, but she shrugged it off. "I went to see someone. She gave me medicine. She says it could take a week or so before I start to notice any differences, but I already do feel a little better."

I had a feeling it wasn't the meds making a difference. I didn't really want to have this conversation right now, but we needed to hash it out or else things would be awkward between us forever, and I didn't want that.

I gestured toward a couple of stools at the food counter, and Avery nodded. "Are you feeling better because of Aiden?" I asked once we sat down. I kept my voice as neutral as possible, but it still sounded a little strained.

Avery nodded again. "We made up."

"I noticed."

"He actually had this great hypothesis about finding acceptance. I was trying to forget about him, but people don't forget about their deceased loved ones. They make peace with them being gone. I needed to make peace with Aiden. I needed closure."

Closure? It didn't look like closure to me when they showed up holding hands, but whatever. If it made her feel better. "I'm happy for you."

Avery frowned at the false note in my voice. She put her hand on down on my arm. "I'm sorry I pushed you away."

I didn't know what to say, so I started folding my pizza receipt into a tabletop football.

When I didn't respond, she apologized again. "I'm sorry, Grayson."

"I know, Aves." I sighed and kept my eyes trained on the paper football. I couldn't look at her. If I did, all of my resolve would crumble.

"I'm too late, aren't I?" Avery whispered in a trembling voice.

The guy behind the counter slid three large pizzas in front of me, but I totally ignored it.

"Too late for what?"

Avery stared at her lap, and I barely heard her next

words. "You said you'd wait for me."

"What?" I was so shocked I almost fell off my stool.

Avery mistook my question for confusion and started to ramble out an explanation.

"I know that was a long time ago. I know you usually have a short attention span where girls are concerned, and I know I lasted longer than all the girls before me, but I was sort of hoping you meant what you said about giving me another chance once my heart was all fixed."

"But...but..."

I'd never looked so incredibly un-cool in my life. I couldn't pull myself together. I just sat there sputtering words like a stammering idiot. I'd been so sure things were done between us. She had Aiden back! How could she be standing in front of me right now asking for a second chance when the guy of her dreams was right across the room and totally interested in her?

"But I thought you and Aiden were..."

Avery processed that and then gasped. "Is *that* why you've been acting so strange? You think Aiden and I are together?"

"You guys went out on Saturday." It was dumb to feel jealous about that, but I did anyway.

"It was part of our science experiment."

I resisted the urge to scoff at her. "I've got news for you, Aves. When a guy says he wants to take you out *in the name of science*, he's totally full of it. He really just wants to take you out."

"But you've taken me out like a million times for the

experiment. You kissed me once *in the name of science*."

"Exactly."

Avery scrunched up her face. She was so adorably clueless I almost kissed her again right then and there. Instead, I crossed my arms and said, "Aiden likes you. He didn't take you out on Saturday just to help you finish your science experiment."

Avery's face smoothed back out. "I know." She sighed. "We had a good talk. He apologized. He explained a lot of things to me that I really needed to hear." She shrugged her shoulders and held out her hands in a gesture of surrender. "I forgave him."

"And that's all?" I had a sneaking suspicion there was more to it than that. Aiden was too pissed at me Saturday morning not to have tried anything.

"We kissed," she admitted. A soft layer of pink rose in her cheeks, but it wasn't the normal overwhelming red that usually overtakes her face.

I didn't realize my jaw was clenched so tightly until Avery brushed her fingers across it. "We had to Grayson. At least I did. Otherwise I never would have known."

I caught her fingers and laced them in mine. "Known what?"

"That you were right," she said simply. "I'm not in love with Aiden. He's my best friend, and I love him, but I'm not *in* love with him."

I was half tempted to say "I told you so," but that would have been rude. "So what you're saying is there's hope for you after all."

Avery chewed her bottom lip. I was going to have to talk to her about that habit because every time she did it, it got harder and harder for me not to kiss her. One of these days I was not going to be held responsible for whatever actions I was driven to.

I watched her mouth and felt myself starting to crack, but then she lifted her big blue eyes and looked up at me completely vulnerable from beneath her lashes, and I forgot about her lips. I forgot to breathe.

If it had been any other girl besides Avery, I would have known she'd done it on purpose in an attempt to kill me on the spot. The fact that she was completely unaware of the effect she had on me made the moment that much more maddening. I was done for.

"No," she whispered. "I'm saying that I hope there's hope for *us*."

The only way to describe what happened next is the word attack. I totally attacked her. Hands and arms and lips and tongue. I fused us together so fast she probably didn't even know what was going on until the first time I let her up for air.

Her face was all flushed, and I was panting hard and smiling like an idiot, but I didn't care. "I'd say there's more than hope for us, Aves."

I brought my lips down to hers again—with slightly more self control this time, thankfully—but we were interrupted before I could kiss her. Levi and Brandon were standing there, all scowls and rolling eyes. "I thought we came here to bowl. Are you guys coming or what?"

I tightened my grip around Avery. "Bowling is overrated."

"Seriously?"

Avery laughed at the annoyance in Levi's tone. "Bowl our first frames for us," she told him, never letting her eyes leave mine. "We'll be there in a minute."

"And take these pizzas with you," I added, so glad that Avery and I were on the same page at the moment.

Brandon sighed and picked up one of the pizzas, but Levi groaned. "It's not even your turn! Owen and Libby have both disappeared too."

"Wait." My hands finally fell away from Avery's waist. "*Owen and Libby* are missing?"

I glanced at Avery in shock, but she didn't seem as surprised. She had an amused gleam in her eyes that told me everything I needed to know. "No way!" I said. "This I have got to see."

I jumped off my stool and dragged Avery with me, completely forgetting about the pizzas I'd ordered. Hopefully Brandon and Levi could manage all three of them.

"Check the arcade. Libby has a thing for photo booths."

I stumbled to a stop and blinked down at Avery. "Are you serious?"

Avery laughed and then pointed toward the entrance to the arcade. There was a photo booth there, and it was definitely occupied by someone—or someones—very enthusiastic about getting their picture taken.

"No way," I said again when Avery and I came to a stop in front of the booth.

The heavy breathing and slurping sounds had to have been somebody else.

"Okay," Owen said, releasing a low moan that made my mouth fall open in astonishment. "You can tutor me in math. But absolutely no clothes with cats on them when you come over. It's creepy."

"Clothes are irrelevant," Libby rasped. "And unnecessary."

Just then something hit the curtain, and Owen's shirt fell to the floor. The kissing sounds increased. When I heard the sound of a belt being undone and another deep groan from Owen, I looked at Avery and said, "Shouldn't we stop them?"

To my surprise, Avery shrugged. "If anyone can handle Libby, it's Owen."

She reached for the strand of pictures that were being spit out of the machine and raised her eyebrows so high that I felt compelled to rescue my best friend. I snatched up the shirt off the floor and then pounded on the side of the booth. "Yo, Owen! Did you want me to go ahead and bowl for you or what?"

I laughed at the panicked string of curses that came from my friend's mouth.

Libby emerged then, somehow managing to look completely dignified, even as she straightened her shirt and ran her fingers through her messed up hair. She smirked at my shock and plucked the string of pictures from Avery's hands. "Yummy," she said, heaving a shudder, and then walked away without another word.

I stared after her until I heard the curtain slide open. Avery had pulled it back. Owen was sitting there flushed red, lips swollen, hair mussed, with an odd look of both awe and horror frozen on his dazed face.

I tossed him his shirt. "You okay there, tiger?"

Owen blinked at the sound of my voice, and after he slipped his shirt back over his head, he looked up at Avery. "There is something seriously wrong with your friend."

We both laughed as he scrambled to his feet and practically ran away from us.

I tugged Avery to a stop when she started to head back to the group. At her questioning look, I made a suggestive nod toward the now-vacant photo booth.

Avery turned the most adorable shade of red yet. "I really think we need to get back to the group."

"Fine." I sighed so dramatically that Avery laughed. "But if I win, then you have to agree to be my girlfriend."

Avery took my offered hand and gave me a very knowing smile. "And if I win, then I get to be."

Epilogue

Avery

The science fair was so different this year, and it was all because of the guy standing next to me. Grayson looked amazing all dressed up. Although he agreed to wear some nice slacks and a dress shirt, he simply could not, under any circumstances, be coerced into tucking the shirt into his pants. He also wore his tie so loose around his neck it was practically a necklace. And then there were the sneakers. Of course, being Grayson, the entire outfit made him look like a Hollywood hipster instead of a slacker.

He was actually causing quite a stir among the crowd of science geeks. Many girls had taken much longer than necessary to stop and check out our project. The rumors of the hottie obviously spread as the day went along, because the traffic at our table got heavier and heavier.

It didn't help that Grayson absolutely loved the attention. He was the star of the 2013 Utah State Science Fair, and he totally knew it. He stood there laughing with strangers and telling stories of our adventures—always making them sound much more dramatic or romantic than they really were. Every time someone would sigh, giggle, or gasp, he would flash me that special dimpled smile and then turn up his charm and win them over even more.

Eventually the judging committee got around to us, and it was time for us to present our project to them. People must have been waiting to hear everything in detail, because a large crowd gathered around us. I'd never seen one project garner quite so much attention before.

I was a nervous wreck, same as I was every year, except worse because of all the extra attention. Luckily, Grayson was there to help me out every time I got choked up from my anxiety. One small squeeze of his hand and my head would clear and I could focus again. I honestly could never have presented such a personal project without him.

Finally, I got to the last stage of grief, and I suddenly had twice the support. I took Aiden's hand and he grinned at me—a smile every bit as beautiful as his brother's.

"And to show the success of my project, I have brought the proof of my acceptance," I said to the judges, pushing Aiden forward. "I'd like you to meet Aiden Kennedy—the boy who shattered my heart, and my very best friend in the whole world. As you can see, by experiencing the seven stages of grief, I have finally accepted what happened between us and have forgiven him completely."

"Even if I don't deserve it," Aiden added, earning a round of chuckles from our audience.

I gave him a hug. He said he was sorry one more time and everyone clapped.

"A very impressive project, Miss Shaw," one of the judges commented.

I was about to say thank you when Grayson stepped up next to me and said, "Impressive, but still incomplete."

The judge who'd spoken to me—as well as the rest of the judging panel—was now watching Grayson with a curious expression, waiting for an explanation.

I couldn't help sending him my own startled look. I didn't know what he was up to, but I sincerely hoped he had a plan because if not, he might have just ruined our chances at placing in this fair.

Grayson winked at me and then turned his smile on the judges. "It's true that Avery has proved she's gone through the seven stages of grief and reached acceptance over what happened. However, if you read her original hypothesis, her intent was not to reach acceptance, but rather to cure her broken heart. Avery has not yet proved that her heart is cured. Would you agree?"

A low murmur swept the crowd, and a few of the judges were now frowning. "What are you doing?" I whispered, starting to panic.

Grayson answered my question louder than necessary. "I'm finishing the experiment, Aves."

I glanced at the judges, and while I felt only confused, it was clear that they were all intrigued.

"You're going to prove that my broken heart is cured? Right now?" I asked just to clarify.

"Nope. You are."

"Me? What? How?"

Grayson didn't answer me. He turned and addressed the crowd. "Ladies and gentlemen, please, if you will, gather around. I need your help in order to prove Avery's theory a success."

The crowd scooted in closer and went silent, holding their breaths in anticipation. I admit I was among those who'd stopped breathing as I waited for Grayson to get to his point.

Finally, he turned to me and said, "You believe your heart is completely cured, right?"

"Yes?" I said slowly.

Grayson's smile spread wide across his face, but the look of mischief in his eyes frightened me. "Prove it," he said.

"Prove it?"

"Yeah. Right now."

"Um…?"

Was he *trying* to make me have a major anxiety attack?

"If your heart was still broken, you couldn't be in love again, right?"

"Right…"

Grayson turned fully to me then and took my hand in his. "Avery."

My heart leapt in my chest at the use of my full name.

Grayson almost never used my full name.

"In case it isn't obvious, over the course of this experiment I have utterly, and completely, fallen for you."

I gasped. When I sucked in a breath, it was so loud it felt like the walls rumbled. It took me a second to realize that was because *everyone* had gasped right along with me.

He couldn't have said what I thought he just said. There was no way. Grayson Kennedy did not fall for girls. They fell for him. Still, he was looking at me, and there wasn't a hint of a play anywhere on his face.

"What?"

Grayson took both my hands now and gave them a squeeze. "Somewhere between the shower and the Red Bull I fell in love with you, Aves. I'm talking epically. There is no coming back from a fall like mine."

I heard a number of sighs from the crowd behind me, but I barely registered the fact that we had an audience. My brain was suddenly in overload thanks to all the blood my out-of-control heart was pumping to it.

Grayson stepped so close to me that our faces were mere inches apart. He put his hands on either side of my face and calmly said, "Breathe, Aves."

I hadn't realized I'd stopped.

When I took a breath, he smiled at me. "I love you." He let go of my face but held my hand again and faced the crowd. "I love her," he said. "Like crazy. And now that I am no longer an impartial, objective, outside observer in the Avery Shaw Experiment—because I assure you I care very much about the outcome of this particular test—I need all of you to stand witness and judge for me whether or not Avery's heart is indeed cured."

Grayson looked at me again and said, "Tell me you love me back. Admit it to the judges and your friends and Mr. Walden and our parents and all the other random science geeks standing here right now. Prove to them that you, Avery Shaw, are cured because you are every bit as in love with me as I am with you."

Grayson stopped talking, and his audience waited, heart in hand, for my answer. And then, something not very uncommon for me happened. I burst into tears.

Don't worry. They were definitely happy tears. Grayson was right. I hadn't realized it until that exact moment, but I was absolutely in love with him.

I laughed through my tears and smiled so big at Grayson that he scooped me into his arms. "I am definitely cured," I told him.

Grayson grinned but shook his head at me. "I think I need to hear the actual words to really be convinced."

It was my turn to shake my head. "Has hanging out with nerds taught you nothing? You're a kinesthetic learner, Grayson. You don't need to hear it, you need to actively participate."

I threw my arms around his neck and kissed him. I mean really, really kissed him. Tongue and all! In front of the judges and our parents and my friends and my teacher and every other random science geek in the state of Utah.

People around us cheered and clapped and whistled like crazy. It should have caused me to have a major anxiety attack, but thanks to Grayson and how much he'd helped me, all it did was make me laugh so hard I had to break our kiss.

"I love you, Grayson," I finally said.

"I love you too."

Grayson kissed me again and then laughed as he spun me to face our audience. "What do you think? Is she cured?"

I didn't need the crowd's cheer to know I was cured, and from the smiles on their faces, the judges didn't either.

Epilogue #2

(Whatever, I make my own rules!)

Grayson

This is more of just a PS, really, because somebody had to tell you that Avery and I TOTALLY KICKED ASS at the science fair last year. We took first place and got this huge trophy that put all my basketball ones to shame. I wouldn't let them display it at school because it had my name on it next to the words "science fair," but after I graduated, I broke down and gave it to Mr. Walden to put in the glass case outside the office.

As first-place winners, Avery and I both won partial scholarships to the colleges of our choice. Can you believe it? Me? A *science* scholarship? (In your face, geeks of the world!) I used it toward my first year at Utah Valley University where I made the basketball team. Owen made the team too and came with me. Now we're teammates *and* roommates. It's pretty sweet.

It sucks being away from Avery, but Owen and I drive back to Spanish Fork almost every weekend. He still won't admit he's dating Libby, but there's no other reason for him to go home every weekend, so he's not fooling me.

Avery will be joining me at UVU next fall, while Aiden has decided he's more of a University of Utah guy. Works for me. He and I never fully recovered from The Great Aiden/Avery Fallout of 2013. Not that we hate each other, and we weren't exactly BFFs before, but I think as long as I'm dating Avery, things will always be a little awkward between us. And considering I don't plan to ever stop dating her, he and I have just learned how to bear one another's company.

Aiden and Avery's relationship is solid, but it's not the same as it was before. She'll survive his absence just fine. Plus, she'll have me to keep her occupied. And boy do I have all kinds of plans to keep her plenty occupied! *insert evil grin here* Next year is going to be awesome.

Oh! And just in case you were wondering…I'm totally majoring in social science.

ACKNOWLEDGEMENTS

Just a quick thank you to all the usual suspects. To my husband, the most amazing man in the whole wide world, thank you. I love you. I couldn't do it without you. Thank you to all of my family—my parents, my brothers and sisters, and my kids. You are the best support system anyone could ever ask for!

Thank you to my beautiful beta readers, all the book ladies, and my editor, Sandra Udall. Together you all help me take my hot messes and turn them into something readable. Heaven knows I couldn't do that all on my own.

And especially thank you to all of my wonderful fans! If you didn't love my characters as much as I do, I'd probably stop creating them. Here's hoping you love Grayson as much as I do. I wrote half of this book from his point of view just for you guys!

CPSIA information can be obtained at www.ICGtesting.com
Printed in the USA
LVOW07s1931240215

428161LV00010B/866/P